WENDY M. WILSON

Lying Under Water

Contents

Preface

The dry weather which has for some months past been experienced in Manawatu broke on Thursday night, and since that time till the present (Monday, noon) there has been a heavy fall. As a consequence, a great deal of the country is at present lying under water... Manawatu Herald, Volume II, Issue 60, 23 March 1880

1

Out of the Creek

Awahuri, New Zealand, November 1880

A pair of cold, dead eyes stared up at her, the irises milky and expressionless. She pressed her heel onto the creature's gills, below where the pitchfork had entered, and pulled it out. It took some effort as she'd stabbed down with all her strength to make sure she killed the monster. She bent over and caught her breath as a wave of nausea passed through her, then straightened. She needed to keep cheerful for Joey. He was already in a panic about their perilous situation.

Another of the monsters lunged at her, fangs bared, and she squealed and swatted at it with her pitchfork, backing away before it could latch its teeth onto her ankle. "Get away from me you bloody beast."

She nudged the dead eel onto the sled with the tip of the pitchfork and put the pitchfork beside it. "I don't know how you can eat these things, Joey. I couldn't eat anything that looked at me like it wanted to kill me."

Mette Hardy's adopted son Hohepa, known since his adoption as Joey, prodded the oily skin of the eel with his finger. "I love eels when they're cooked. They taste so good. I don't like them when they're alive, though." He looked up at her, grinning. "Am I allowed to say bloody? I thought you said…?"

"No. Of course you can't. Sorry Joey. I was scared when the eel came at me."

"Are we going to catch any more?"

Mette contemplated the writhing mass of eels that had wriggled out of the flooded creek and onto the road, looking the way she imagined hell would look. "One will do for now," she said. "Let's get back to the house. It's getting late. Frank will want his lunch." She'd been going to say, don't touch the eel, the blood will kill you, but decided against it. No use putting any more bad thoughts into Joey's head. She'd get it into the fire and cooked as soon as she could. The blood of a cooked eel was perfectly safe. No need for him to worry about being poisoned, on top of everything else.

She grabbed the ropes of the wooden sled and dragged it towards the farm gate. Joey followed behind, bending down to keep the eel and the pitchfork in place. "What are we going to do if we run out of food?"

"We've got enough in the larder to last a week." Mette said. "We'll probably get sick of eating the same thing every day, but we won't starve. There's always more eels, and Frank could catch an owl or a wild pig."

"But the flood might last longer," said Joey. His face was screwed up with anxiety. He worried about everything these days. He'd been such a lively boy when she first met him, but he'd changed since the fire. She was reminded of Frank, who woke in the night with nightmares about what he'd seen when he fought in the Land Wars. Joey insisted on staying close to her and refused to let her out of his sight. At least Frank wasn't affected during daylight hours, and she could usually keep him calm at night when he awoke with night terrors.

"Miss Anderson at Sunday school said that Noah's flood lasted forty days. Forty days and forty nights, she said…"

Mette unlatched the farm gate and dragged the sled through. "I doubt the flood will last for forty days. Those kinds of things only happen in the Bible, never in New Zealand that I know of."

"Like someone who lives for seven hundred years?"

"Exactly like that. Do you know anyone older than a hundred?"

As she closed the gate, she thought she heard something. A long wail, like the sound of a ship in fog, but higher pitched.

"What was that?"

"Somebody yelling?" suggested Joey helpfully.

The wail came again.

"It came from behind the stable," said Joey. "Maybe the horses…."

"It was human," said Mette. Leaving the sled where it was, she grabbed Joey's hand and ran around the stable to where the creek now flowed. It had not been on their property at all until yesterday, when the eel-laden water had burst over the banks, throwing up leaves and branches and dead animals.

The sound came again, closer this time. Someone was calling for help.

She raised her skirt and stepped along the muddy bank, her boots squelching in the mud, knowing if she stumbled into the water she'd be swept away. Joey grabbed her skirt from behind and followed her.

"Be careful, Mumma. Don't fall in."

"If I do, you run and fetch Frank. You'll have to, Joey."

Fifty yards away, around a bend, they came upon an over-turned carriage, a fancy open Landau with black and gold doors that must have cost a small fortune. The horse was still attached but had been dragged onto its side by the current. It was holding its head above the water, kicking, and trying to get some purchase on the stones.

"Is someone there?"

A head rose from behind the carriage: a man with a trim dark beard shot with grey, his hair plastered over his forehead. He was clutching the door of the carriage with one hand. "Ah, thank the Lord. We were crossing the stream and the water capsized the carriage. My wife…"

"Is she with you?"

He nodded. "She's down here by the wheel. I have hold of her—for now. Do you have a man with you?"

Mette glanced at Joey. Not much use sending him for Frank. He wouldn't leave her side, especially if he thought it was someone else in danger.

"My husband is too far away. But I can help you," she said. "Joey, go into the stable and bring the rope hanging on the wall."

He hesitated, looking at her fearfully.

"Go on. Be quick. I'll wait here. I won't move, I promise."

He crept cautiously back along the bank, stepping in the muddy footprints Mette had left, glancing back now and then as if to make sure she hadn't fallen in and been swept away.

She looked around for a good tree to tie the rope to. "I'll throw you a rope and pull you in," she said to the man in the carriage.

He grimaced. "But aren't you…?"

4

"Yes, I am," she said. The baby was still for once, but she was confident she had the strength to pull this man and his wife to safety without harming her baby. Joey would help. He was only ten, and small for his age, but he had some strength in his wiry arms.

"What's your name?" she asked, raising her voice over the thunder of the water.

"Burns," he said. He moved his elbow awkwardly, trying to get a better grip on the carriage door. "Jeremiah Burns. My wife is Grace. And yourself?"

"Mette Hardy," she said. "My husband and I have a horse farm up there — you can see the stable through the trees. I'll take you there when I get you out."

Joey was gone for less than five minutes and came running back with the rope dangling from his hand. "I got it, Mumma."

"Right. We're going to tie one end around this tree and then throw the other to these people. Then we - you and me - are going to pull them in."

"Are you sure you're able to tie a rope?" asked Burns, his voice rasping with tiredness. "I don't want to be swept away before anyone can help me. My farm hand was driving us and went in the water when we flipped over. I haven't seen him... he probably drowned."

She ignored him and concentrated on the knot. She'd spent the first twenty years of her life in Haderslev, a port city in Denmark, where every school child was taught how to tie a knot. And Frank had shown her how to tie knots for horses, which was important now she lived on a horse farm. She passed the rope around the tree and made a figure eight, then made a bow loop on the other end.

"Are you ready? I'm going to throw it to you."

"Are you positive it's tied tightly enough?"

"You'll have to trust me." She gritted her teeth. "Here you go." She spun the rope above her head a couple of times, and then sent it sailing in his direction.

Holding onto the side of the carriage with his elbow, he lunged at the rope with his free hand, missing it by inches.

"Could your wife hold herself for a bit so you can get the rope with both hands?"

He ducked out of sight, then reappeared holding on to his wife. She was a pale woman, wearing a dark dress and bonnet that shielded her face; she looked liked a drowned cat. He hoisted her up and draped her over the board in a position that looked very uncomfortable to Mette. She lay there limply, not helping herself.

He reached his hands towards her, holding his wife steady with his elbows. "Throw it again, quick, before she slips away."

Mette threw the rope again, and this time he caught it. He slipped the loop over his wife's shoulders and around her waist.

"Ease her into the water on this side of the carriage. Joey, you stay with the rope and hang on tight in case it breaks. I'm going down to where she'll hit the bank at that curve. I'll try to pull her in."

Burns sat astride the carriage and lowered his wife into the water, still not letting her go. The water between his wife and where Mette was braced to catch her was spinning around like churning butter.

With a sudden heave, he threw his wife towards the bank. "Here she is."

His wife tumbled downstream for a few seconds, then stopped with a jolt as the rope tightened. She looked like a rag doll that someone had thrown into the water, not a human. Mette held on to a branch and leaned out as far as she could, managing to grab hold of Grace Burns' skirt. She braced herself on the bank and held on to the skirt with both hands, gradually gaining ground until Mrs. Burns was in the shallow water at the edge. Once she had her on the bank, she took off the rope and tossed the end back to Joey, who caught it easily. Mrs. Burns lay still, coughing up water but not moving.

Pounding Grace Burns on the back, she called out to Joey. "Throw the rope to Mr. Burns"

Mr. Burns struggled on top of the carriage. "Let me release the horse first."

He crawled out onto the front of the carriage and tugged at the traces. In minutes, the horse was standing free, bracing itself against the torrent, stepping in place trying to keep its balance. Then the water overcame it; losing its footing, it was swept into the deepest part of the water and rolled away downstream. Burns watched it disappear.

"Drat," he said. "We'll have to look for it later. It's a strong horse. It might survive. Throw me the rope. I'll pull myself in. I don't want you to hurt yourself."

Joey had reeled in the rope and looped it around his arm, in the way that Frank had taught him. He threw it to Mr. Burns, who grabbed it and dragged himself towards the bank without Mette's help, pulling hand over hand on the rope, his head bobbing up and down in the water.

Water dripping from his clothing, he hurried over to his wife and shook her. "Grace. Grace. Are you still with me?"

She moaned and rolled over, vomiting water. He cradled her head in his lap and stroked her hair. "We're safe, Grace. We're both safe."

"Can you carry her up to the house?" asked Mette. "I have

a coal fire going in the kitchen, and she looks as if she needs warming up."

Burns hoisted his wife in his arms and followed Mette to the house, grimacing with the effort and the lack of help from his wife, who lay across his arms with her arms dangling limply over his. Once in the kitchen he set her on a chair near the fire and began rubbing her hands. She stirred and spoke for the first time. "My baby...is my baby safe?"

Mette put her hands on her own belly. "Is she...?"

He rubbed his eyes, not looking at Mette. "Not as far as I know."

Grace Burns sat up abruptly. "My baby was in the water. She was swept away." She gazed at Mette, her eyes bright. "You saw her. You must have seen her."

Mr. Burns took his wife's hand in his. "Now dear. Don't upset yourself again. Jane has gone, and she's not coming back."

He turned to Mette and said quietly, "We lost a little girl last year. She hasn't got over it yet. She sometimes thinks she's still alive and in another room."

Mette felt a kick from her own little girl. She sat down abruptly. "How terrible."

"She just wants to die," he said. "But I'm not going to let her. She won't get away with it this time."

Mette did not know what he meant. Had she died before? How was that possible? And why did he think he could stop her from dying?

2

In the High Paddock

Frank Hardy could not believe how exhausted he was. He remembered his time in the army when he'd been on forced marches, carrying his full kit in the worst conditions imaginable: the humidity and flies of India, the dry heat in Crimea, and the rain, mud and mosquitoes of the Land Wars in New Zealand. Now, after a day of hard physical labour he was done. When this was over he'd better start lugging a heavy pack over rough ground at double time to get himself back into condition.

For now, he had to force himself to keep going, to be ready for what was coming. The district had been inundated with storms for days, and now the rain had eased he'd heard a rush was on its way down from the hills. He estimated it would hit the farm within the next twenty-four hours.

His leg muscles were starting to cramp and his back ached from all the bending he'd been doing. The only thing that kept him going was knowing how short a time he had left to protect Mette and the boys. Marriage was more complicated than he'd realized, and adopting a ten year old and taking in his older brother to live with them had changed Frank's life. But he dreaded the thought of losing any of them. On top of that, he was already overdrawn at the bank and had borrowed money from his brother-in-law; this flood could finish him.

He'd carried bales of hay from the stables up to the high paddock, making sure the water trough was full of fresh water, and dumping bucketfuls from the pump into the butt beside the kitchen door. The pump would be useless in the flood, and both animals and humans would need drinking water. They could soon be totally marooned, with the creek running through the house. He planned to bring his few remaining horses up to the high paddock at the last minute and have a tent ready for Mette and the boys before things got too dangerous.

Hemi, his adopted son Joey's older brother, had gone into town on Copenhagen, Frank's horse, and Frank was not sure if he'd be back before the next surge hit. Hemi was a hard worker and keen to learn, as long as he could learn what he wanted, not what Frank felt necessary. Frank had asked him not to linger in town, which almost guaranteed he'd take his time. He wondered if he'd run into the same problem with Joey when he was older, or with his own as-yet unborn son. He hadn't been the best of sons himself and hadn't written to his father in England for years.

When Frank and Mette had adopted Hemi's younger brother, Joey, they'd asked his brother Hemi if he wanted to be a Hardy as well, and he'd said no; he was a Maori, and he wanted to stay that way. And he wasn't going to change his name, either. Mette had suggested that he would still be a Maori and could keep his name even if they adopted him, but that had not gone down well. In theory, his grandmother in Palmerston was still his guardian, but she was old and frail, and did little more than give him the occasional shilling to spend when he was in town. Both the boys and their aging grandmother had been forced from the Pa - the Maori village - when it the chief had sold it to the government.

From the rim of the high paddock he could see floodwaters covering the countryside all the way to Feilding, ten miles away. It looked deceptively calm: the water sparkled and small islands thrust up at intervals, some with animals grazing on them. A few canoes and flat boats shuttled around trying to rescue sheep and cows before the next rush of water arrived. But the idyllic scene from his farm masked the unseen view of the swollen carcasses of farm animals, and furniture that had washed from houses, property losses that were going to cause financial devastation. He wouldn't be surprised if there were bodies out there as well. They would appear when the floods subsided.

Immediately below him, the O'Halloran farm was starting to succumb to the water. James O'Halloran, like Frank an ex-soldier, had a small dairy operation, with a dozen good Ayrshire milking cows and an Ayrshire bull, which he hired out as a breeder to other dairy farmers in the area. His farmhouse and barn were above the waters for now, but that wouldn't last. The house would be underwater up to the window sills before the floods had passed. Frank had offered to help O'Halloran and his son Niall bring his cows up to the high paddock. He planned to go down to the farm after lunch and help them.

For now, it was time to head back to the house for lunch and to check on Mette. The baby wasn't due for a couple of weeks, but he didn't like leaving her alone more than a half day. He worried constantly about what he would do if the baby came early. Could he deliver it himself if it came to that? The thought scared him: he'd had more experience with death than he had with life.

Mette was leaning against the stable wall eating an apple, one foot propped back against the wall, rubbing her belly with her free hand. She was looking down and didn't see him coming at first. He stopped on the path and watched her, wishing he could paint. She looked like something done by Millais—he vaguely remembered a painting of his he'd seen in a library somewhere—a portrait of a milkmaid. After a few minutes, she glanced up and saw him standing there.

"Frank. There you are. I was waiting for you. I thought you'd be hungry by now."

Once, not so long ago, she would have run to him and thrown her arms around him. Instead, she stayed where she was, her face drawn. The pregnancy was draining her, he could tell, and he felt guilty for putting her through it.

He leaned beside her and took her hand.

"Are you feeling alright? You look pale."

She nodded. "I haven't stopped all morning. I've got anything that could be ruined up as high as I can—the baby clothes, all my books…"

"Of course," he said, smiling. "But don't overdo it. Could you rest this afternoon? I have a couple of things I still need to do, but we must surely be prepared by now…why don't you lie down for a bit? We can manage with the supplies we have for a week."

"Not any more. We have two extra people now. I found them in the creek earlier in an overturned carriage. They'll have to stay until the water goes down."

"Someone we know?"

"No. Grace and Jeremiah Burns. They thought they were taking a short cut to Feilding and capsized by our gate. They had a farm hand with them as well, but he got washed away. Look out for his body when you're down at the O'Hallorans place."

"There'll be more bodies before this is over," he said grimly. "But we need to think about the living for now. Another three people will be coming back with me this afternoon. I'll bring up some supplies from their house. Anything you need?"

"Tinned food," she said. "Potatoes. We're a bit low, although I have kumaras. Onions. I have enough flour for a month. We have a good-sized slab of bacon, but if they have some we could use it. Joey and I got an eel this morning. There are dozens of them coming up out of the floodwaters. I started a fire in the yard and it will be done in another hour."

"I thought I smelled something cooking. Are there still apples in the stable? If there are, I'll grab a couple and head back down to O'Halloran's place. I'm not up to socializing with anyone right now." He eased his position to help the ache in his lower back. "Send Hemi down to help when he gets home. And Joey if he can tear himself away from your skirts."

Mette sighed. "Hemi's already here. They're in the soddy doing something they don't want me to see. Smoking pipes, I think." She pulled a letter from the pocket of her skirt. "Hemi brought this from town. He stopped off at Mr. Snelson's store. I don't know why it was sent there, but…it's from…"

Frank stared at the envelope. He was tempted to toss it into the fire with the eel. A letter from his son, or from someone writing on his behalf. He'd made his son's grandfather a promise that he'd never go to the South Island if Milo never

13

came to the North Island. He'd hoped they'd never see each other again.

In the end, he tore it open and read it quickly.

He handed it to Mette. "He's coming here."

"Here? Oh no…"

"Not to Awahuri. He's being sent to the front at Parihaka. He's a second lieutenant now, and they've asked him to lead the local volunteer force. He wants me to know that I won't see him. Not if he can help it."

"I thought the war plans were on hold. Does this mean you'll have to go as well?"

Frank shrugged. "It's looking increasingly likely that I'll be sent to Parihaka, especially if they're bringing men up from Otago. But not yet." He took the letter and shoved it in his pocket. "We have to get through this mess first." He smiled at Mette. "Can I have a kiss before I go back to work? I need something to get me through the last two or three hours."

She obliged. After several minutes, she moved him away. "That's enough. You're starting to squash the baby."

"He's getting in the way in the daytime as well as at night," he said, grinning. "Will he be coming soon, do you think?"

"Two weeks," she said firmly. "She's patient, unlike her father."

* * *

Although they'd been expecting him, he couldn't rouse anyone at the O'Halloran's farm. The dairy herd grazed quietly in the home paddock, and supplies were piled on the verandah, but no one answered his knock or his cooey.

He pounded on the door. "O'Halloran? Are you there?"

His knock sounded hollowly within the house. He opened the door, his fighting instincts on high alert, hoping he wouldn't find anything wrong. "O'Halloran?"

The house had four rooms, with a hallway running straight back from the door to an attached washhouse. The first door to the right was ajar, and he peered in. A pale grey shawl had been tossed on the chesterfield; a pair of grey embroidered slippers sat on top, as if the owner had recently left the room. In the hallway, two pairs of men's shoes were placed in a neat row. The O'Hallorans, father and son, had apparently put on their boots in the hallway when they left the house, leaving their shoes behind.

Had they gone out on the farm for some reason? He tried the other doors. The first two opened, one to a small parlour, the other to a bedroom. But something blocked the third door. It moved an inch, then stopped. He pushed harder and it moved slightly. What was there? A sack of something? A body? Why would someone leave a body lying behind a door? On the other hand, why would someone leave a sack of anything there?

"Hello? Anyone there?"

His voice echoed hollowly around the house. Feeling somewhat foolish, but worried, he shoved the door as hard as he could. It moved another inch or two, but not enough for him to see inside. Through the crack in the door he thought he could see something, but there wasn't enough light to be sure.

A horse whinnied nearby. The O'Hallorans arriving home? Reluctant to be discovered prying inside the house, he pulled the door closed and went back out on the verandah.

A carriage horse, its traces hanging on the ground, stood

in the yard, its head lowered, swaying from side to side. Its coat looked damp. Frank approached the horse cautiously and picked up the traces, shortening them until he held the horse firmly near the head.

He stroked its mane and said softly, "What are you doing here then? Did you come from another farm?" It had come down the creek, he realized suddenly. This must be the horse that had been pulling Jeremiah Burns' carriage. Mette had told him to look out for the body of the farm hand. But that would have to wait while he took care of the living. What was behind the door was another thing, however. He was curious.

"Let's go around to the back of the house and see if we can look through the window of that room," he said to the horse, who looked back at him nodding gently, as if it agreed completely.

Taking the horse by the bit, he pulled it along after him as he went around the side of the house to the back. The creek had risen to the edge of the building, and was flattening the blue hydrangeas that surrounded a natural terrace below the windows. He could not tell how deep it was or whether there was a slope under the surface. He vaulted onto the horse and forced it into the water. It moved forward reluctantly, lifting its feet high like a show horse and clumping them down hard onto the surface of the bushes.

He calculated that the room with the blocked door would be the first window he came to. But it was no good. He knelt on the back of the horse and held on to the window frame, but the room was dark and he could see nothing. He tried opening the window, but it was locked from the inside and he was unable to budge it.

16

He was returning to the front of the house, thinking he would go through into the house and find the rear door, when he heard horses approaching at a canter.

In minutes, two horses arrived in the yard, bearing O'Halloran, father and son. James O'Halloran was a tall, gaunt man, clean-shaven, with hair parted on one side and worn long and flat, cut just below his ears. As usual he was dressed in a dark suit and tie; he reminded Frank of the itinerant preachers who arrived in town regularly. From what he knew of the man, he sported a similarly pious affect as the preachers, and like them it was a front for a hard, intolerant man.

O'Halloran jumped down from his horse. His son stayed on his horse, looking surly. Frank recognized the expression. He'd seen it a lot lately on Hemi's face.

"Sergeant Hardy. Sorry I wasn't here to greet you. We had some business in town."

In the middle of the flood? It must have been important business. "Never mind," said Frank. "I just arrived. I found this horse in your yard. I believe it came down from our place. My wife rescued a couple earlier today who were thrown from their carriage near our gate. I'm expecting a body to…"

He saw the younger O'Halloran, Niall, flinch as if he had been struck.

"…to surface soon. Mr. and Mrs. Burns had a farm hand with them, and he was swept away when they when they fell out."

"No time to look for him now. We'd best get these cows up to your paddock. And the supplies." O'Halloran turned to his son. "Niall, load up your horse with the supplies on the verandah. Be quick now. We need to get everything done before night fall."

Frank could see Hemi plodding reluctantly down the hill from the high paddock, his demeanour signalling that he was being put upon. Joey trudged behind him, freed from Mette's skirts for once.

"My boys will give you a hand, Niall," he said. "There'll be a hot meal and a glass of ginger beer ready for you when you're finished." He turned to O'Halloran and added casually, "And your wife? Will she be joining us?"

O'Halloran stared at the ground and shook his head. "We took her into town," he said. "She wanted to stay with her sister until this is over."

Frank nodded. "I see. Well, she couldn't have done better than to stay with us. We have the highest elevation in the district. But her choice, of course." Not the time to challenge the man, he thought. Too much going on right now. But there was obviously more to the story than O'Halloran was telling him. When he had more time he would insist on an answer.

As they rounded up the dairy herd and ushered them slowly up the hill, he looked back at the O'Halloran house. No one was there, he knew that. But the feel of the door when he had tried to open it, he couldn't forget that. Something had stopped it. Or someone. In the light spilling from the hall through the crack in the door he was sure he had seen the edge of a nightdress. And O'Halloran had claimed, against all reason, that he had taken his wife into town.

3

Three Families

Mrs. Burns was resting in the spare room claiming she felt ill and had a headache that could only be cured by sleep. Mette had made up the bed with the eiderdown quilt the Danish women from the clearing had sewn for her as a wedding present. It had been stored in the trunk she had brought with her from Haderslev for two years, a prized possession she loved. But Mrs. Burns did seem unwell, and she certainly needed the warmth of the quilt. Mette's fervent hope was that she wouldn't vomit on it and ruin it.

Mr. Burns had gone outside to chop wood after first attending to his wife. He'd been in the bedroom for quite some time before coming out with a grey, worried face.

"How is your wife?" Mette asked, visions of a ruined eiderdown in mind.

He sighed. "Not well. I'm afraid she hasn't been able to shake off the loss of our daughter. She's sad much of the time."

Mette put her hand on his arm. "How old was your little girl?" She'd seen so many babies and young children die; most women she knew had lost at least one child, usually before their second birthdays. They were so fragile when they were small. She worried about her own little girl—if that was what she was carrying. Frank was sure it was a boy because of the way the baby kicked him in the night.

"A year and a half," said Burns. "Our little Janey. She'd just started walking, and her teeth were all coming in. It was the teething. That's what took her, unfortunately."

Mette wanted to tell him about how willow bark helped reduce pain, but it was probably too late for that. If she came to know Mrs. Burns better she'd tell her about the usefulness of willow in helping to dull physical and mental pain. She had her own little store of crushed bark in the top cupboard, ready for when she would need it. She didn't intend to suffer through childbirth the way her sister had. And she wanted to take something that was safe, not one of the popular medicines used by so many women.

She'd promised to make one last meal before they were forced to move up to the tents in the high paddock. She had decided to make a good mutton stew with lots of carrots and parsnips and, because she had plenty of apples in the store, some apple dumplings for pudding. She wanted everyone to be well-nourished before they had to start sleeping on hard ground in draughty canvas tents.

She went out to the stables to get the apples, passing Mr. Burns in the yard. He had chopped enough kindling to last for several days, but was still working determinedly at the chopping block, his face red and sweaty. She hated to stop his efforts, but it was a rather a waste of his time.

"Frank has already taken enough wood up to the high paddock for us to keep a fire going for a week," she told him.

"You really don't need to chop up any more."

He let the hatchet fall to his side. "I'm sorry. I feel as if I should be doing something."

"You'll be busy tomorrow getting us all settled up in the high paddock," said Mette. "You can rest for now if you like. There'll be so much to do tomorrow."

He nodded. "We'll have to start early. Look at the sky over the ranges."

Mette shaded her eyes and looked to the east, where a long line of ranges split the lower half of the North Island into two parts. She could see a massive bank of dark clouds sitting above the hills. "Oh my goodness. It's so black. Do you think it's going to rain again?"

"I would say so," he said. "The rush coming down tomorrow afternoon will be followed by another one soon after. We're in for a rough few days."

Mette wasn't sure if it was because of what Mr. Burns said, or something else, but she suddenly felt as her body was being dragged downwards from the inside. She took a single slow step and stopped, looking frantically at Mr. Burns. Just as suddenly, the feeling went away and the baby started kicking at her ribs vigorously as if she was doing a hand stand.

"Are you alright, my dear?" asked Mr. Burns. He dropped the hatchet and took a step in her direction.

"I just felt strange for a moment, but it passed." A sudden whiff of stomach-turning charred flesh reminded her of the eel she had left baking in the ashes of the fire. "Actually, if you want to be helpful, there's an eel in the fire that needs chopping up. Could you do that for me?"

"Of course. Should I use the hatchet?"

"I'll get you a knife and a bucket."

She brought him one of her good ivory-handled carving knives, and a large billy can and went back inside to prepare the mutton stew and to roll out the pastry for the apple dumplings. She was stirring the stew and feeling slightly queasy at the thought of eating it when he came through the door carrying the billy can overflowing with small chunks of cooked eel.

"The boys will be very happy to see that," she said. "They love eels."

"I'm rather fond of eels myself. Not in this form, but when I was a young man in the East End of London we used to eat jellied eel. Street vendors pushed carts up and down the streets selling little pieces of eel in glasses, cooked in broth that had turned into jelly… I remember…"

He stopped abruptly and turned towards the bedroom door. His wife had screamed.

"Your wife…" said Mette. She dropped the spoon and walked quickly into the bedroom with Mr. Burns behind her. Mrs. Burns was lying on her back, arched up on her elbows, her eyes wide, her body shuddering.

Mette lost all her English skills. *"Mein gut! Hvad er der med hende?"*

Mr. Burns sat on the bed beside his wife, pulled her to him and began to stroke her hair.

"Grace my dear, I'm here. You're safe now."

Grace Burns began to sob. "I need, I need…"

"What does she need? What can I get for her?"

Mr. Burns shook his head sadly. "She needs her medicine. We were on the way to the dispensary in Feilding to get her some when we were swept away. I wouldn't have gone out in this weather otherwise, but it's been very difficult for her, the poor woman."

"What kind of medicine does she take? Perhaps we have something…" They had no medicine in the house, other than a bottle of whisky from which Frank sometimes drank when he awoke with a nightmare. But the willow bark was there in her cupboard.

He took a few minutes to answer, rocking his wife in his arms and trying to quieten her. Eventually he turned to Mette. "Tincture of Opium. Laudanum. She's always had it in the house for when she felt low, but since our little girl died…"

Mette had heard about laudanum. Several women she knew swore by it for toothache. But she preferred her own little mixture, which she felt was much safer than laudanum, and worked better as well.

"I have something that might help," she said. "A cup of tea with some honey—there's a row of manuka bushes near here, and I get honey from bees who have their hives nearby. I stir some ground up bark of the willow tree into it. I dry it myself and pound it up with a pestle…"

He looked doubtful. "That sounds foolish to me," he said. "Tree bark and honey? Who taught you to make that? Some old wife?"

Mette contained her irritation. "No. I learned about willow tree bark from an old family friend in Denmark. He was a scientist. He called it salicine and said it was the poor man's quinine. And the honey makes it easier to digest. Honey comes from bees, just like milk and butter come from cows. I'm sure God intended us…"

Mrs. Burns gave another cry, pushed herself away from her husband, and fell back on the bed, shaking.

"I suppose it wouldn't hurt," he said cautiously. "Willow bark and honey, both things that God created, so surely they would not hurt her."

"I'll bring her a pot of my tea mixture, then," said Mette, wondering if he'd heard about the blood of uncooked eels, which God had also created. "And some thinly sliced bread with a scrape of butter, to help her sustain herself until she's able to get out of bed. She'll need to take care of herself tomorrow." She started to leave the room, then remembered something. "Did you bring the knife back in? It was a wedding gift, and I'd hate to lose it."

"I think I left it outside on the chopping block," he said. "I'm sorry. I'll fetch it as soon as my wife settles down."

* * *

She was making apple dumplings when the boys came down from the high paddock bringing Niall O'Halloran with them. She'd never met him or his parents and was somewhat shocked to see a nasty red mark on his cheek. She had no problem giving the boys a swat on their bottoms if they were naughty, but a slap on the face that left a mark was wrong. Frank said his own father had beaten him and his brother with a belt when they misbehaved, and the sons of his father's employer, who had gone to Rugby, had tales about being caned by prefects—older boys who helped teachers with discipline—when they caused trouble. She had convinced him that pain like that would lead to more trouble; she did not want him to punish Joey and Hemi at all. Their lives had been hard enough and what they needed now was affection, praise and kind words.

"Is Frank finished yet?" she asked.

Hemi shook his head. "Sergeant Frank said to tell you he'd be about half an hour. He's helping Mr. O'Halloran bring the cows up to our paddock." He sniffed. "Are we having mutton stew? I love mutton stew."

"We'll eat as soon as Frank and Mr. O'Halloran get here. Hemi, would you hop outside and get my carving knife? Mr. Burns left it on the chopping block. He was chopping up an eel."

Niall O'Halloran had been staring at the floor. He raised his head and sighed. "I'll go if you like, Mrs. Hardy."

She watched as he left. He was not a happy young man. She could tell from the slump in his shoulders that something was bothering him.

He returned holding the knife with both hands. "This is a nice knife. Where did you get it?"

She took it from him, wiped it with a cloth, and opened the knife drawer. "It was part of a pair I was given by Lieutenant Monrad and his wife as a wedding gift. They're made by Mappin & Webb...they're the best you can buy. And they cut extremely well, and Frank keeps them nice and sharp. Even I can cut the Sunday joint easily."

Niall touched one of the blades, staring at it intently. "The blade is really sharp. Does Sergeant Hardy sharpen it very often?"

"Every time I use it, almost," said Mette, smiling at him, hoping she could cheer him up by talking to him.

"What are the handles made of? Is it bone?"

"Ivory. It comes from elephant tusks."

Joey came over to inspect the knives. "Elephant tusks? Are the elephants dead when they cut off the tusks?"

25

Mette had not thought of that possibility before. "I'm not sure. They must be. You wouldn't cut tusks off an animal when it was alive, would you?"

The boys were unconcerned about that, clustering around to touch the knives and test the sharpness of the blades.

"We should take these up to the paddock when we go up there," said Niall. "You know, in case there's rats or possums hanging around."

"We might want to get rabbits as well," said Hemi. "But I have a rabbit gun. We can take that."

"You should get your dad to buy you a jackknife," said Niall to Hemi. "Then you could be ready for anything."

"He's not my dad," said Hemi. "He's my brother's dad. Anyway, I'd rather have a rabbit gun. Then I can get the rabbits from a distance. A lot of rabbits."

The whole thing was starting to sound like one of Joey's penny dreadfuls or boys' own adventure serials. "We won't need any weapons," said Mette. "And if we want to catch a rabbit Frank will have his Barlow knife with him. It's no use shooting them if you mean to eat them. You'll end up with too many pellets in the body."

That sent the boys off into an excited discussion about how to catch and skin a rabbit, so Mette gave up. At least they were happy about the idea of living in the wilds of the high paddock for a few days.

The door opened and Frank came in with Mr. O'Halloran.

Mette hurried to greet them, shutting the door behind them. "Careful, Frank. You're letting out all the warmth."

He took off his coat and handed it to her. The coat felt cold and damp, but she was happy to see he looked ruddy and healthy, and less tired than he had earlier in the day.

"Mette, this is Mr. O'Halloran from the farm below us. I see you've already met his son Niall."

Mr. O'Halloran nodded at Mette. She felt him looking her up and down, assessing her youth. He turned to Frank. "Your second wife then? And these two boys are from your first? You were married to a Maori woman, I see. Or not married. I know how these things work."

Frank frowned. "Mette is my first—my only—wife. And the boys are adopted. They were living at the Pa with their grandmother when it was bought by the government and they had nowhere else to go."

O'Halloran took off his coat and dumped it into Mette's arms, on top of Frank's coat.

"Thank you for taking us in," he said to Frank.

Frank glanced at Mette and raised his eyebrows slightly. "My wife is happy to help," he said. "I'm sorry your wife couldn't join us."

"Second wife," said O'Halloran. He took a seat beside the fire, settling comfortably into Frank's favourite armchair. "My first died in childbirth years ago. Sarah arrived from Connemara a few months ago. A young woman, like your wife. She's a distant relation of my late wife. Happy to come out here into a settled situation like mine. You know how things are in Ireland these days."

Frank brought him a glass of beer and sat beside him on a stool, warming himself in front of the flames. "Where are the other two?" he asked Mette. "Mr. and Mrs. Burns, did you say?"

As if on cue, the bedroom door opened and Mr. Burns came out.

"She's asleep," he said to Mette. "That concoction of yours

27

did the trick."

"Good evening, Burns," said O'Halloran.

Burns stared at O'Halloran without speaking, his face rigid with dislike, and then turned and went back into the bedroom.

"Mr. and Mrs. Burns are staying with us as well," said Mette to Mr. O'Halloran, exchanging a puzzled glance with Frank. "Have you met before?"

O'Halloran nodded. "Not under the best of circumstances, I'm afraid. But I'm sure we'll get along very well. We'll make sure our tents are far apart, and Mr. Burns and I will try not to come to blows."

Perhaps Frank should take the ivory-handled carving knives with him to the high paddock after all. Of course, he was not likely to leave his new Colt Single Action behind. His rifle was locked in a cupboard in the bedroom, but he usually kept his Colt handy. They'd be well protected from any villains or wild animals and would not need to take the carving knives with them. And he was much stronger and more experienced in a fight than the other two men, and could keep them apart if necessary. She'd seen him in action and was sure of that.

4

Bedtime Story

Frank relaxed in his arm chair by the hearth, and watched Mette reading a chapter of the Bible to the boys, her nightly habit. O'Halloran had offered to make himself useful by feeding the horses, and the Burnses, who had taken dinner in their room, appeared to have settled down for the night. The sound of light snoring echoed from the bedroom.

Joey snuggled in beside Mette on the sofa, while Hemi sat cross-legged on the floor playing with his knucklebones, pretending he wasn't paying attention. Frank had cleaned some sheep knuckles for him and he carried them in his pocket at all times. Playing with the bones helped him ignore the rest of the family, who tolerated the game until the clicking became too annoying.

Hemi would mature eventually. For the moment, Frank was more concerned about Niall O'Halloran who sat with his back to the fire, chin propped on his knees, and stared at Mette with a strange expression on his face. Frank thought it might be admiration - even adoration. He knew the feeling. The red weal on Niall's face was hidden in the shadows thrown by the

29

fire and candlelight. The mark was fresh, and Frank wondered how he'd got it. Had he seen something happening to his step-mother? Had he done something with his stepmother, not much older than him, and been punished by his father? Watching him, Frank decided that when he had an opportunity he'd go down and look behind that bedroom door and see what was stopping it, even if it meant breaking the window.

He was about to look away from Niall when the boy suddenly looked at him. He held his eyes for a minute and Frank was sure he wanted to say something - to tell him something. Then he sighed deeply and put his head down on his arms, his face hidden.

"Joey, would you get a book from the bookshelf please?" asked Mette, closing the Bible. "Time for a story."

"You said you'd read *The Water Babies*," said Joey. "Should I get that?"

Mette glanced at Frank. He could tell what she was thinking. A book about a poor little chimney sweep falling into the river and drowning might not be the best choice for tonight, especially not for Joey.

"What about *Westward Ho!*" he suggested. "An adventure story is always a good choice."

"Too old for Joey," said Mette. "Joey, why don't you choose something?"

He came back carrying three of his favourite penny dreadfuls, probably the two Frank had seen him stealing from Mr. Robinson's Book Shop in Palmerston a few months ago. One was about Dick Turpin the highwayman and his horse Black Bess; Turpin was shown on the cover grinning evilly while he flourished a brace of pistols. The other book was an even worse choice: *A String of Pearls*, about a mad barber who cut off people's heads and put them in pies. Frank was not sure he wanted to hear that one, considering his own past experiences with people losing their heads. The third book was a paean to British royalty, about the beauty and courage of Queen Victoria. Not the thing to read to two young Maori boys who'd been thrown from their home by representatives of that same monarch.

He saw Mette glance at him again, reading his thoughts as she often did. "I'll read you this one," she said to Joey, taking *Dick Turpin* from him.

Joey listened to the story with rapt attention.

"That was really good," Joey said, when Mette finished. "When I grow up, I'm going to be a highwayman."

Hemi paused in his game, the knucklebones resting on the back of his hand, and eyed Joey. "A highwayman? You're too scared to get on any of Sergeant Frank's horses. How're you going to be a highwayman? Will you run after the coaches like a dog?"

Joey's lower lip trembled and he stared at his brother, his eyes filling with tears.

"That was uncalled for, Hemi," said Frank. "Joey has ridden Copenhagen several times. He can't ride as well as you can, but very few people are able to."

"I think it's time for you boys to go to bed," said Mette. "We'll all have a lot of work to do tomorrow. Niall, you can sleep out in the soddy with Hemi and Joey. There's a spare mat out there you can use, and you have a blanket, don't you?"

The boys out of the way, she leaned back and sighed. "I'm so tired and my back is aching. How will we get through the next few days?"

31

Frank sat beside her and put his arm around her shoulders. "Why don't you go to bed? I'll wait for O'Halloran to come back in. I'll give him a whisky before he goes to bed. He isn't going to find the floor of the library very comfortable. He'll need something to numb the pain."

She leaned against him. "I'm too tired to move. I think I'll sleep right here."

"Don't move then. I'll carry you into the bedroom." He lifted her with some effort. "God, you're getting heavy. How much does this baby weigh?"

"It's not all me and the baby," she murmured into his chest. "There's other things in there...water, and..."

"Don't tell me," he said. He eased her through the bedroom door, turning sideways. "You'll ruin my romantic mood."

He put her on the bed—the same bed with the latest spring mattress that Mette's sister, Maren had given them with her inheritance—and pulled the cover over her. "You can warm up the bed for me. I won't be long." He sat on the edge of the bed and put his hand on her belly. "You've changed shape. Did the baby move?"

She nodded and rolled onto her side, facing him with her eyes closed, her hand on his thigh. "Maren said the baby..."

The muffled voice of Mr. O'Halloran, speaking loudly and angrily came from outside.

"What do you think you're doing? Get away from that fire."

Frank leapt to his feet. "He must be talking to his son. Did you see that red mark...?"

"On his face? Yes I did. You'd better go out and make sure he doesn't hit Niall again."

More yells from outside. "Oh no you don't. I know you. I know who you are, what you did..."

They heard grunting and the sound of a slap, followed by a muffled yell.

Frank blew out his cheeks. "Right. I'll separate them. I'll take my bat with me."

He grabbed his cricket bat from the chest at the end of the bed, and strode outside into inky blackness. O'Halloran was standing in the yard in the ring of light that emanated from the coach lamp he had taken out to the stable. The wind had picked up, causing the candle in the lamp to flicker, making the shadows bob and weave like demons. As his eyes became accustomed to the dark, he realized there was a figure huddled below O'Halloran. The bastard had gone after Niall again.

"Niall? Are you hurt?"

"Sergeant Frank, what's going on?" said Hemi from the doorway of the soddy. His voice sounded shaky.

"It's Mr. O'Halloran and his son," said Frank. "Don't worry. I'll sort it out."

"It's not me. I'm over here," said Niall O'Halloran. "With Hemi. Is my father hurting someone?"

The person on the ground sat up and groaned. "I was washed away in the creek. I've been trying to find someone to help me and I saw the candles inside your house. And then there were some slices of eel in the fire and I thought…I was hungry…"

"It's Arthur," said Mr. Burns from the doorway. "My farm hand. Arthur, are you alright? I was sure you had drowned." He hurried forward and grasped Arthur by his shoulders.

"Wet. Cold. Hungry," said Arthur. He tottered to his feet with Burn's help and looked at O'Halloran. "Why were you shaking me? I was just trying to get something to eat."

O'Halloran stood there breathing heavily, saying nothing. Then he turned on his heel and stamped back into the house.

Frank went to Arthur and helped Burns pull him to his feet. "Come on inside. We have some warm food and blankets. I'll throw some more coal on the fire. You can stay here, although I'm afraid all I have left to offer as accommodation is the stable."

"That would be nice," said Arthur, his voice feeble. He put his arm over Frank's shoulder. His hands were freezing. Frank could feel his bony chest through his shirt. The man needed feeding, not just because he hadn't eaten for a day, but because clearly he hadn't eaten well for months.

Inside, O'Halloran had helped himself to Frank's whisky and was standing with his back to the fire. Frank assisted Arthur to the sofa, sat him down, poured another glass of whisky and handed it to him.

"Drink this. And put that blanket from the back of the sofa around your shoulders."

"You're wasting good whisky on the man," said O'Halloran. "He's a farm hand."

Arthur gulped down the whisky and held the glass out to Frank, who refilled it for him.

"I'll get you a plate of mutton stew," he said. "I believe there was some left over. And some bread."

"Have some sympathy for your fellow man, O'Halloran," said Burns, who had followed them back into the house. "What happened, Arthur? We've been here for hours. I'm sorry I didn't come looking for you, but you were swept away so rapidly, and Grace…"

"I can swim a bit." Arthur pulled the blanket more tightly around his thin shoulders, glancing between Frank and Burns. "But I went head over heels all the way to that farm below this one banging myself all the way down. I was barely able to drag myself out of the water, and then I passed out on the bank.

When I woke it was dark. I couldn't see a thing, and I could hear dogs howling in the distance. I was scared, so I stayed near the creek until I found the spot where the carriage flipped. I came up the road to the gate—it was hard, it's so dark—then I saw the candlelight and climbed the gate, and…" His teeth started to chatter loudly, and he put his hand on his mouth to muffle the sound.

Frank sipped his drink and watched Arthur. He was not a young man. He must be at least thirty. He had light sandy whiskers, and was dressed in a threadbare blue serge coat and a floppy, wide-brimmed hat which he'd somehow managed to keep hold of during his descent. A Londoner, and from a modest background by his accent. The son of a grocer, perhaps, or a railway clerk. Not the kind of person you found working on a farm, although in New Zealand your background often made no difference to where you found yourself. How did he end up working for the Burnses?

An awkward silence fell. "We'd better all get to sleep," Frank said finally. "We'll need to be up and working at first light. Burns, will your wife be able to manage by herself tomorrow?"

Burns nodded. Frank saw him cast an angry look at O'Halloran. "She'll be better after a good night's sleep. I'll be awake early, I always am, and I'll make sure everyone gets up."

"I spent fifteen years in the army," said Frank. "I won't have any trouble waking up. Drop a feather on the floor of my room and I'll be out of bed and standing at attention before you can say Dick Turpin." Some light humour might ease the tension in the room, he thought.

"I can make the same claim," said O'Halloran. "Twenty years for me. The Irish Guards, including a stint at the Palace." He looked at Burns, his mouth turned down. "I'd say it will be up to you and me tomorrow, Hardy. The only two real men in this group."

Burns gave an angry "Humph," and took hold of the coach lamp. "Come, Arthur. I'll escort you out to the stable. Take that blanket with you."

Arthur followed him meekly out the door. Frank sighed and went back into the bedroom where Mette was fast asleep. He dragged off his shirt and trousers, folded them on the chair ready for the next day, and squeezed in beside her. She was radiating heat; he wrapped his arms around her and fell asleep, his mind spinning with questions. What was going on between Burns and O'Halloran? Or O'Halloran and Arthur for that matter? And who was Arthur? Why was he so thin, bordering on skeletal? Had the Burnses not been feeding him?

5

Setting up Camp

Mette awoke the next morning feeling better than she had for weeks. Frank was already up and she could hear him directing the boys in the yard as he readied the horses for the trip up to the high paddock.

They didn't have as many horses as they used to. Frank had sold his new mount, John Bull, to pay for feed, and gone back to riding Copenhagen, saying she still had a year or two before she needed to be put out to pasture. They also had a broodmare they called Dolores, and a running-at-foot yearling colt they were hoping to sell next May at the York Farm sales in Marton. For a short time they'd owned a pony and trap, but that had gone to Mette's sister, Maren, who'd told her privately that Frank had used it as security for a loan from Maren's husband Pieter. Frank didn't know she knew.

Dolores was in foal and due in another six weeks. Frank had been supplementing her feed with bruised barley mixed with bran to build up the bone and muscle of the foal, which had been sired by Dead Shot, one of the best thoroughbreds in the colony. Frank's hopes for finally making money for them were pinned on the high price he might get for Dead Shot's offspring, but a prolonged time up in the high pasture with feed supplies dwindling might put those hopes in jeopardy.

She pulled her dress over her shift and wrapped a shawl around her shoulders. She'd have to wear the same clothes until they could get back into the house, and she wanted to be warm at night. Even with spring coming, the nights were still cool. She'd given up wearing a bonnet not long after she'd discovered she was with child and wore her hair in a single braid which she twisted into a bun when she wanted it out of the way. Frank teased her about her hair looking like Dolores' braided mane, especially amusing to him when they were both, as he liked to say, in foal. But she didn't mind. Listening to Mr. Burns and Mr. O'Halloran the previous night had made her appreciate Frank and his jokes all the more.

Mr. and Mrs. Burns were sitting at the kitchen table, Mrs. Burns wrapped in Mette's precious quilt. The colour had returned to her face, but her expression remained sad and she refused to engage Mette in conversation.

She sliced Mr. and Mrs. Burns a large slab of bread each and gave it to them with butter and marmalade. Mr. Burns chewed his food unappreciatively, his eyes fixed on his wife. He was worried about something. Did he think she would deliberately choke herself on the bread?

Mr. Burns finished chewing his bread and wiped his lips carefully on the clean napkin. "Do you have a wheelbarrow? I'd like to convey my wife up the hill."

"Could she not walk?" Mette was annoyed, imagining her quilt pressed into the dirty wheelbarrow as it jiggled and joggled around. "We need the wheelbarrow to carry up some of the supplies. I was going to fill it with food from my larder."

"I can walk, Jeremiah," Mrs. Burns murmured. "If Mrs. Hardy can manage in her condition, I'm sure I shall manage as well."

"Perhaps you can sit on one of the horses," said Mette. She was about to offer Dolores as a mount for Mrs. Burns, but stopped herself. Frank wouldn't allow anything that had the smallest chance of harming his broodmare. He'd rather let Mrs. Burns crawl up the hill on her hands and knees.

She went outside, followed by the Burnses, Mrs. Burns holding on to her husband's arm and looking a little more cheerful. She could not help wondering if Mrs. Burns might be happier if her husband treated her less like an invalid and more like a useful member of society.

Frank was loading Copenhagen with bags of oats and barley and greeted them with a quick nod before turning to the boys, who were hovering nearby, unsure what to do with themselves.

"Hemi, take Copenhagen up to the paddock, unload all this and put it in the supply tent. Then take her to the grazing area in the pasture. Not near O'Halloran's fence though. He says he's laid poisoned oats along the fence line to stop the rabbits destroying the grass and I don't want my animals near any poison. Niall, go into the kitchen and help Mrs. Hardy load up the supplies in the wheelbarrow and wheel it up."

He glanced at Mette. "And don't think for a minute you're going to push it, Mette. You can walk up with Mrs. Burns and decide where we should put everything. Take the billy cans with you. O'Halloran is up there milking his cows and most of the milk will be going to waste. Collect as much of it as you can. "

"What should I do?" asked Joey. "I can carry something."

"You take up the billy with the eels," said Mette, before Frank could say anything that would hurt Joey's feelings. "It's heavy, but you can manage."

Joey grinned happily. "Should I get the knives as well?"

Frank frowned. "What knives?"

"Never mind," said Mette. "We were looking at my carving knives last night, and the boys thought we could use them to defend ourselves."

Frank patted his pocket. "I have my revolver, Joey. If you get attacked by an enraged rabbit, I'll kill it, don't worry."

Joey looked crestfallen. Mette was wondering if she should say something to cheer him up when a tall thin man with a long, narrow face came out of the stables, yawning and stretching. He was perfectly at home for someone she'd never seen before.

"Who's this?" she asked Frank.

Mr. Burns stepped forward and laid his hand on the man's shoulder. "This is Arthur, my farm hand. Arthur, this is Mrs. Hardy who saved us from the creek and has kindly offered to put us all up for the duration of the flood." He smiled at Mette. "Remember I told you my farm hand was caught in the rush and I thought he'd drowned? Fortunately, he didn't. He appeared after you'd gone to bed last night, safe and sound although somewhat damp and hungry."

Arthur gave Mette a half salute. "Morning Mrs. Hardy. Pleased to meet you. Wish you could have saved me as well, but never mind."

"We're about to take everything up to the high paddock," said Frank to Arthur. "Get yourself a piece of bread from the kitchen. And then get all the blankets you can carry and bring them out here. We can throw a few over Dolores and you can carry the rest."

It was starting to drizzle, and they could see sheet lightning in the clouds over the ranges, as they made their way up the track to the high paddock. Mette and Mrs. Burns had wrapped extra blankets around their shoulders and each carried a billy with cutlery rattling inside, held partly in place with Mette's supplies of baking powder, salt and mustard. Frank had a pack of tools and equipment on his back and escorted Dolores carefully, making sure she didn't step into a hole or stumble on a muddy clump of grass. Mr. Burns' farm hand walked on the other side of Dolores, holding a pile of blankets in place on her back, his other hand free. Apparently he didn't feel the need to contribute more than that, and Mette was surprised that Frank hadn't forced him to carry more. Mr. Burns had been given the task of escorting the colt, not an easy thing to do as the colt was lively and butted against its mother if left alone. Burns kept it on a short leash, seeming to know what he was doing.

As they walked up the west side of the lower paddock, Arthur struck up a conversation with Frank. "Nice place you got here, Sergeant Hardy. Lived here long, have you?"

Frank always enjoyed the company of men, especially working men. It was one of the many things Mette liked about him.

"A couple of years," he answered. "I drove a coach out of Palmerston before that. Left the army back in sixty-nine when my regiment returned to England and I was with the Armed Constabulary for a while. But I grew up with horses. My father was head coachman on a large estate. I could have started as a stable boy on the estate, but I preferred to join the army. I was looking for adventure."

"That explains why you speak a bit posh," said Arthur. "And

41

did you find it?"

"Did I find what?" asked Frank. He was leaning forward, his eyes fixed on the track in front of him, watching where Dolores placed her feet. She plodded along taking one ponderous step at a time, her belly hanging down awkwardly.

"Adventure," said Arthur.

"Some," said Frank. "I'm still finding it, although things have been calmer recently."

"Where did you serve? India, I suppose?"

"Of course. But Crimea first. Then India."

"And you never served in England? Or Ireland?"

"I was at Aldershot," said Frank. "For my training. But apart from that I haven't been in England for well over twenty years."

"So you left in 1860 then?"

"Thereabouts," said Frank. "Of course, now I'm a New Zealander. I've been here forever." He pulled on Dolores' reins. "Watch your step there, Arthur. This part has washed away."

"I noticed that when I came down last night," said Arthur. "Just about killed myself."

"Hard to see in the dark," said Frank. "I thought you said you came up on the road on the other side of the creek?"

"Did I?" said Arthur. "I was in the bush and then I wasn't. I don't remember where I was, to tell you the truth. There was water…and…then I was on a track. I just kept coming towards the light."

They were silent for a few minutes, then Frank asked, "How long have you been in New Zealand?"

"Just a couple of weeks. I lived in Australia for many years. But I needed a change so I came here."

"And how long have you worked for Mr. Burns?"

"A week," said Arthur. "I met Mr. Burns at a pledge meeting in Foxton, and he was kind enough to offer me a job."

"A temperance meeting?" asked Frank. "In Foxton? Why Foxton?"

"What do you mean why Foxton? It's close to where he lives. He has a property in Himatangi just outside Foxton. He isn't there much. He spends his time giving talks around the country about the sins of liquor, and he wanted a man on his property when he was away."

"He said he was driving in to Feilding to..."

Mette interrupted him before he could mention Mrs. Burns' laudanum problem and wonder aloud why Mr. Burns needed to drive to a more distant town to get the medicine when they lived close to an equally large town with a dispensary. "Do you think it's going to rain before we get to the tents, Frank?" It was a silly question but all she could think of in the instant to stop him.

Frank took the hint and began talking to Arthur about the weather.

Mrs. Burns did not appear to have heard. Her face was raised and her eyes closed, a look of pure pleasure on her face as the mist settled on her cheeks.

"Mrs. Burns? Grace?" said Mette. "We're nearly there. Are you managing? Would you like me to carry your billy?"

Grace Burns opened her eyes and smiled at Mette. She was a pretty woman when she smiled, and the fresh air had added colour to her face. "It's been so long since I've been out in the rain. I'm enjoying it. I grew up in Wellington, you know, and it rains all the time there. I love the feel of rain on my face."

* * *

Mette's energy was fading fast by the time they finally settled in the high paddock. Mrs. Burns was resting in her tent, and her husband had taken Hemi and Joey to check on the height of the water. Mette set about organizing the supplies in the tent, kneeling awkwardly with the canvas drooping inches above her head, steam rising from her dress and shawl. Her dress tugged across her belly and she couldn't find a way to be comfortable. When she couldn't stand it any more, she crawled out of the tent and found Frank waiting outside.

"All done?"

She sat on an empty Teacher's whisky crate that had been filled with tins of sardines and packages of corned beef. "I know we've hardly done anything yet, but I'm really tired. I thought I'd manage better than this."

He knelt in front of her, concerned. "I should have taken you into town before the water got so high. I'm sorry. You've been so strong and I've taken you for granted. What can I do to make you feel better?"

She leaned against him. "I'll sit for a while, and then I'll start preparing tea. I don't need any help. You have so much to do - and so much rests on your shoulders - I'll be fine."

"You're a trooper. Where are the boys?"

"Hemi and Joey went to check the creek with Mr. Burns. They're going to bring back some kindling to start a fire. I'm not sure where Niall is. I sent him to take the billies up to his father and bring back some milk. He should have returned by now. Do you think they went down to their house?"

"I hope not. The water's rising. It'll be getting dangerous." He stood up. "I think I'd better go and see what they're up to. Something isn't right with the O'Hallorans."

"The mark on Niall's face, do you mean?"

"More than that." He hesitated. There was something he wasn't telling her, but she knew better than to push him. If he suspected something about Niall and his father he would tell her if he thought she needed to know.

6

Death in the Pasture

To reach the place where O'Halloran had left his herd, Frank took the track along the fence separating their two properties. His neighbour had spread a layer of oats boiled in arsenic along either side of the fence to kill rabbits - successfully, apparently. On Frank's property a thick stand of Toi Toi grass and flax would keep his own animals away from some of the danger, but he could see a line of dead rabbits - as many as forty or fifty - scattered beside his fence. He took out his Barlow knife and speared them through their ears, flipping them off his property. He wasn't taking any chances that his horses would investigate the dead rabbits, even though they almost never ate meat. He'd come back later when he had more time and shovel the poisoned oats back onto O'Halloran's property, where they belonged.

O'Halloran's dairy herd was grazing in an open area of good pasture surrounded by bush. The cows milled around nibbling at the grass, but many of them had heavy udders and had clearly not been milked. There was no sign of either O'Halloran or Niall, although two empty billy cans sat to one side. Niall had been here at least.

He walked around the outside of the pasture calling O'Halloran's name. No answer.

Unless the O'Hallorans had gone back to Frank and Mette's house for some reason, they must be on their own property somewhere.

He jumped the fence and went down the hill to the O'Halloran's house. The creek had risen higher since yesterday and was lapping at the verandah steps. He was squelching his way across the yard when Niall came out the front door. He looked worried. "Sergeant Hardy, have you seen my father? He hasn't done any milking and I thought…"

"What were you doing in the house, Niall?"

"Looking for him. My father, I mean. I checked the barn and the stable. I didn't think he was down here, but where else would he have gone?"

"And you're sure he's not in the house? Do you mind if I take a look?"

Niall looked at him, puzzled. "Why? I looked in every room."

Frank elbowed his way past him through the front door and checked the rooms again. When he came to the blocked door it opened easily. No sign of a nightdress or a body. The room was small, with a dresser, a bed and a commode - a cheerless room. Beside the bed lay a book on animal husbandry - The Complete Farmer - opened face down. Niall's room, obviously. The window was partly open, and he crossed the room and leaned out. Below him, the water was almost up to the window, flattening the hydrangeas; the grassy area was under a foot of swiftly-moving water. If anyone had shoved a body out through the window it would have swirled away in an instant. He leaned out further and noticed a sack of something lying beneath the window. Not a body, as far as he could tell, but perhaps it concealed a body.

He turned and faced Niall. "Did you throw her body out the window?"

"Did I throw...? What do you mean?"

Frank eyed him, wondering how far he could push the boy. "Before you and your father arrived back from town yesterday I came inside your house. I was looking for you - surprised you'd gone somewhere when I said I was coming down to help with your animals. I tried to open this door and something stopped it. It felt to me like a - like a body."

The colour drained from Niall's face. "A body? Why did you think that? I mean..."

"Niall, where's your stepmother?"

"She went...we took her into town."

"Which is it? She went into town, or you took her into town?"

His shoulders slumped. "She went into town and we followed her. My father said he was going to bring her back."

Frank moved closer to Niall and looked down at him, his hand on the boy's shoulder. "Niall, who hit you? Was it your father?"

Niall pulled away, refusing to meet Frank's eyes. "My father would never hit me." He touched the bruise on his cheek. "You mean this? I banged my face in the barn a couple of days ago. I wasn't looking where I was going and I bumped into a beam."

He was obviously lying, but Frank decided not to pursue it. "Did he hit your stepmother?"

"He was mean to her. But he didn't hit her."

"And at some point your stepmother ran way?"

Niall nodded again and sighed.

Frank was not convinced. The window had not been open

yesterday. And something had been behind the bedroom door. "Let's find your father then, and we can straighten this out."

Niall followed him up the hill to the pasture. The herd had not moved and O'Halloran was nowhere in sight.

"He should be here," said Niall. "Do you think he fell somewhere? Or went into the bush and got lost?"

"Let's go up and walk along the ridge," said Frank. "The bush down here isn't that thick. We may see something from above."

The boy had sharp eyes. They were half way along the ridge, weaving between the cabbage trees, when Niall stopped and pointed downhill. "What's that in the Toi Toi?"

At first, Frank could see nothing. Just a dark patch in the midst of the long grass where he'd walked earlier. He shaded his eyes and the patch became more defined. A pile of clothing? James O'Halloran had been wearing a dark suit.

"Wait here," he said to Niall. He went down the slope to the Toi Toi grass and waded through to where he thought O'Halloran might be.

It took several minutes of thrashing around before he saw a boot, placed at an awkward angle, sticking out from an extra thick clump of grass.

O'Halloran was lying face down, his arms by his side, palms up. If he'd fallen, he'd not made any attempt to block his fall. Frank shook his arm. "O'Halloran?" O'Halloran didn't move. He felt stiff.

Frank put his hands under O'Halloran's shoulders and gently turned him over onto his back.

"Christ!"

O'Halloran was dead, no question of that. As his body flipped over stiffly, a thick flow of blood trickled from his mouth and into his ears. Once, Frank had seen a man survive a bayonet

49

plunged into his neck. That man was lucky; the steel blade had missed the major arteries. But a knife driven into someone's throat the way the knife had been driven into O'Halloran's throat was bound to be fatal. The ivory-handled knife had entered James O'Halloran's neck in the area below his chin, and had been thrust upwards, impaling his tongue, which was thrust out and turning blue.

This was not just any knife. It was his knife, given to him and Mette on their wedding day by Lieutenant Viggo Monrad, the son of the former prime minister of Denmark, a man of unimpeachable reputation. The knife was expensive, part of a set, and it was unlikely that anyone else in the district would own one like it. This knife had come from the drawer in his kitchen. His heart pounded, reverberating in his chest. Death, he was used to. But this one was too close to home.

Niall had come up behind him and was looking over his shoulder. "Sergeant Hardy? Did you find something?"

Frank jumped to his feet and tried to shield Niall O'Halloran from the sight of his dead father. "Don't go near him. He's gone Niall. Nothing you can do to help." He'd not been much older than Niall when he'd seen his first dead body; Niall would not yet understand his own emotions. Years after he'd seen that first body, he saw the head of his own brother hanging from a pole and all the feelings he'd buried over time came out in a rush. The memory still came back, unbidden, when he least expected it.

Niall stared at his father's body, puzzled. "Who's going to milk the cows?" he asked. "If we leave them another day they'll get garget and their teats will... and I don't know how...I don't know..."

His face crumpled and he sat down abruptly, his face white

with shock. "I can't take charge. I don't know what to do…"

"Niall," said Frank as gently as he could, "Don't worry about that now. Let's get your father back to camp. We'll need to protect ourselves, and to find out who did this to him."

"Protect ourselves? You think someone wants to hurt us? Will someone come after me?"

It was hard to know what to tell the boy. Frank glanced back at the body. Better check it out thoroughly before they moved it. "Niall, sit over there on the slope. Don't think about what's going to happen in the future. I'll help you sort everything out later. Right now, I'm going to check your father, to see if the person who did this left a trace of some kind."

Niall didn't move, but squatted down beside his father's body. Frank moved around so he could see him, keeping in mind there was a possibility - even a probability - that the boy had murdered his father. Something had gone on in that house; of the three people who lived there, one person was missing and the other was dead. Only Niall was still here.

Niall's face was a complete blank. He kept his eyes fixed on the body as if he didn't understand what he was looking at. Frank busied himself with O'Halloran's clothing and boots, partly as a distraction. He dreaded the thought of dealing with a distraught youngster. That was Mette's specialty and he was keen to get him back to the camp and under her care.

He searched the surrounding Toi Toi carefully. Nothing. No tracks, no broken or downtrodden stems. Someone must have come from the other side of the fence and not through the grass. Then he checked the body. The face was mottled red with a greenish tinge, which had happened when the body lay face down. The stiffness of the body suggested the man had been dead for a while, as did the un-milked cows. He had seen

O'Halloran early in the morning, and he'd been probably been killed shortly afterwards.

He grasped the handle of the knife and removed it with a sharp tug downwards. No more blood came from the wound. It had clotted, reinforcing his idea that the death was not recent. He wiped the blade on the grass and put it inside O'Halloran's shirt for safekeeping. He felt the anger building within him. Someone had killed O'Halloran with a knife from his own drawer. That meant everyone was in danger, especially his own beloved Mette. He could not afford to let his guard down. He would find a way to get the truth from everyone, starting with Niall, unfortunately. Mette's ministrations would have to wait.

Niall watched, his eyes flickering between Frank and the body. "What can you tell by looking at him?"

Frank moved around the body, staring at it. "Not much. But I wanted to make sure I could describe things to a coroner when it comes to that. Now, we need to get him back to camp. We'll put him in your tent, and…"

Niall looked shocked. "With me?"

"No, no. It looks like it'll be a clear night. You boys can sleep beside the fire. Can you grab hold of his feet? I'll take his head." From that vantage point Niall would be staring into his father's face. If he had killed his father, Frank needed to know immediately. He hoped the look on Niall's face would tell him something, anything, about what had happened.

* * *

Back at the camp, Mr. Burns had a fire going and was feeding sticks into it with the help of Hemi and Joey. Mette and Mrs. Burns were nowhere in sight, and neither was Arthur.

Mr. Burns saw Frank and Niall coming and froze, one hand clutching a burning twig.

"Who…did something happen to O'Halloran?

"He's dead," said Frank. "Murdered. Where is everyone? I want them all here."

Mette crawled out of the Burnses' tent. "She's sleeping…*min Gut*! What's going on?"

"Wake her up," said Frank. "Someone's murdered O'Halloran and I want everyone in the open. Where's Arthur?"

"He went down to the house to get me some apples from the stable."

"Hemi, go up onto the ridge and let me know if you can see him."

"Must I wake my wife?" asked Burns. "Mrs. Hardy just gave her some of her willow bark preparation and it put her to sleep. What happened with O'Halloran? How do you know he was murdered?"

"He had a carving knife thrust into his neck." Frank glanced at Mette and saw her raise her eyebrows and point at her own chest. He gave a slight nod. "You can all sit outside your tents until I return. Niall and I will go down to the O'Halloran farm and look around. See if anything's been disturbed or anyone has been there."

"But we were…" said Niall.

Frank cut him off. "I want to take another look."

"You think someone is on the property?" asked Burns. "Someone must be. No one here killed him. No one had a reason…"

Mrs. Burns' head appeared through the flaps of the tent. Her hair was unkempt and she looked sleepy, her eyes barely open. "What's all the noise about? I was asleep."

Before Burns could give her a softened version of what had happened, Frank said harshly, "Mr. O'Halloran has been murdered, Mrs. Burns. Stabbed in the neck with a knife."

He expected her to scream or react in some overly dramatic way, but instead she turned her gaze on her husband and said sadly, "Oh, Jeremiah."

He shook his head. "No, my dear. No."

Hemi ran back down from the ridge. "Arthur's coming."

"Hemi, did you bring your gun with you?" asked Frank.

Hemi's face telegraphed his guilt. "No. You said I didn't need to."

"Where is it, Hemi? In your tent?"

Hemi nodded. "Sorry, Sergeant Frank. I thought I might need to kill rabbits."

"Get it," said Frank. "Niall, help me put your father in your tent. The rest of you - don't move. If anyone comes, scream."

They put O'Halloran's body in his tent, then flattened the tent on top of him, moving the pegs away further to hold it in place. The canvas would contain some of the smell, at least for a day or so. He'd have to do something about the whole situation before then - find some way of contacting the police. He'd be the obvious person to ride into Feilding, but he was also needed to be here to protect everyone. He could see the group watching him anxiously. Whatever came of this, it was up to him to make it happen.

Niall worked hard, not looking at Frank, concentrating on what he was doing. He'd make a good soldier, Frank thought. He was a big lad, strong, with dark hair and fair Irish skin. Old enough to be useful working the farm with his father. Good-looking enough to attract the attention of a young second wife. And strong enough to kill his father.

Arthur had returned and been informed of the situation. He was unfazed by it all, and stood by the fire eating an apple, clearly no stranger to death. Maybe he could make use of that. He needed a second-in-command.

"What do you want us to do, Sergeant Hardy?" Burns asked. "Shouldn't we send for the police?"

"The water's rising rapidly," said Frank. "Someone can go for the police tomorrow, but it's nearly nightfall, and it'll be a dark night with this cloud cover. In the meantime we're trapped here and I want to make sure nothing else happens. I want all of you seated outside your own tents. Arthur, you sit with Mr. and Mrs. Burns. Joey, you're with Mette. Hemi, give Mette your gun. Mette, keep your finger on the trigger. If you're worried about anyone or anything, shoot in the air."

Mette reached for the gun, but Hemi held it to his chest. "But I thought..."

"Sorry Hemi. But it has to be Mette."

"I don't like holding guns, Frank," said Mette. "Couldn't Hemi take it?"

Frank stared at the two of them, then made a decision. "Alright then. Hemi, I want you to sit beside Mette with your rabbit gun. If anyone moves an inch, shoot your gun in the air and I'll come running. We'll be back in twenty minutes. Now, everybody sit."

They obeyed him quickly. Mrs. Burns held her husband's arm, while Arthur lounged next to them looking bored.

"Let's go Niall."

Niall followed him silently down the slope to the O'Halloran farm. The water had risen even in the last hour, and was swirling in crazy patterns around the steps just below the verandah. In the yard the water was half way up his boots, and he sank down with each step. He estimated he had ten or fifteen minutes to get the truth out of Niall before the water made the situation too dangerous.

The house itself was still clear of the rising floodwaters, and he looked in all the rooms once more. As he had expected, he found nothing new.

"I don't know why we had to come down here again," said Niall, who had followed him into the house. "No one's here. What are you looking for? The murderer? Do you think he's here? Shouldn't I have a gun?"

Frank went back to the front door and blocked Niall's exit. "I wanted to talk to you alone, Niall. Are you sure you've told me everything about what went on here?"

Niall stared past him, watching the water anxiously. "Shouldn't we get out?"

"We've got a few minutes. I want you to tell me what you can while I'm still able to see the inside of the house."

"I told you the truth. What else do you want me to say?"

A loud crack echoed around the yard and a tall black pine splashed into the water in a flurry of branches.

"Niall, what happened here with Sarah, your stepmother? Where is she?"

"She went into town...the water's getting higher. We have to get out." He was breathing heavily, starting to panic. "I'm not a good swimmer. I'll drown. "

Frank turned to look outside. He was beginning to think he'd underestimated the rising waters. But he wanted to push Niall one more time. "We've got a few minutes. Tell me about your father and Sarah. How did they get along with each other?"

Niall clutched on to the door frame, gabbling, his voice shaking. "She hated him," he said. "He made her do things… I heard them in the night. She used to cry out. And he kept telling her she was ugly, and that her family lied to him. She came to New Zealand to marry my father and he was upset when he saw her. He said he thought he was getting someone pretty. She had red hair and he hated that. He called her an Irish peasant."

"And what happened yesterday? Why did you go into town with your father?"

Frank saw Niall's shoulders slump. He was staring at the water but looked like he wasn't seeing anything. "She told him she was having a baby. Yesterday morning. But she said she didn't want it. She said she'd rather kill herself than have his baby. And he…he…hit her. He was really angry. I've never seen him so angry."

"And you tried to intervene?"

"No. I wish I had. I wish I'd hit him back. I didn't. I'm weak. I didn't do anything. Then he left. He went out to milk the cows. She was crying and I sat down on the couch beside her. She said, when he comes back he's going to kill me. And I said, I'll help you escape." He sniffed and wiped his eyes with the heel of his hand. "But we saw him coming from the barn. I'd just left two fifty pound sacks of flour by the door - to bring up to your camp later. So I said to her, go into my room and barricade yourself in with the flour. I took the sacks in and came out, and then she pushed the sacks against the door. I said, you climb out the window and I'll hold him off for as long as I can. I'll tell him you're in my room crying. You make a run for it along the creek. I thought she'd head up to your place, so I told my father she was heading into town. I wish I'd said…"

The water had risen further and was starting to cover the verandah.

"That's good, Niall," said Frank. "Now, let's get out of here."

They were barely clear of the steps and into the middle of the yard when they heard a loud creak and the sound of wood splitting. The house groaned like a human being in pain, then lurched and began to move away from them, sucking water with it. Frank felt the pull - like an undertow in the ocean - dragging at his legs and sucking the dirt from under his feet. He grabbed Niall's arm and dragged him to higher ground. They were almost there when Niall lost his footing and fell, breaking from Frank's grip. He wrapped his arms around Frank's legs and clung to him.

"Help me. Help me!"

Frank took hold of him under his arm pits, lifted him to his feet, and helped him to dry land. The boy was trembling, but he forced away any feelings of sympathy. If he was a killer, giving him time to regain control of his emotions would also give him time to plan his lies.

As they reached safety, he asked, "Niall, did you kill your father?"

"No, no. I swear I didn't Sergeant Hardy. I didn't. My father made me search the creek with him to look for my stepmother. We looked in both directions, and we didn't find her. So she got away. I had no reason to kill him. She's safe."

7

The Water Rises

Mette was strangely calm about the murder of Mr. O'Halloran. He was merely a character in a novel, and she was curious to know how it ended. She'd encountered other murder victims, and had even been in the next room when an old woman was strangled just a few months ago. At the time, of course, she'd been terrified, but knowing Frank was nearby this time made the all difference. They'd had a falling out back then, and she'd had to bear the pain alone. Hemi sitting there holding his rabbit gun was comforting as well. If someone came at her with a hatchet again she would not be able to shoot him, but Hemi would.

Who did Frank think had killed Mr. O'Halloran? Surely not one of their group. He must know something. She guessed he thought Niall was the culprit, which is why he'd taken him down to his farm. She felt sorry for Niall, who did not know what was coming to him. He was probably dangling from an upstairs window right now, spilling the truth about what he had done. But if he had not killed his father he would be terrified, and her heart went out to him.

If it wasn't Niall, it would have to be one of the other two men. She could not imagine Mr. Burns killing someone in a rage; he would be more likely to leave the room in a huff than to kill someone who annoyed him. And Arthur? What possible reason would Arthur have to kill Mr. O'Halloran? Perhaps he'd done it on behalf of his employer, but he'd only been with the Burnses for a week and would surely not have developed loyalty to them that quickly. Unless, of course, they'd hired him to kill Mr. O'Halloran. She'd seen a hired killer before, although when she thought about it, Arthur did not seem the type.

If it was all planned, the Burnses could have been on the way to kill O'Halloran when they turned over in the creek. And meeting him as they did was good fortune for them. But the more she thought of that idea, the more implausible it became.

Arthur was a strange man, however. Not at all like what you would expect from a farm hand. He acted as if he was a guest who did not need to pitch in and help. She'd asked him to get apples from the stables as a way to let him know there were things he could do. He'd come back with a handful and eaten most of them himself. He might actually be too lazy to murder anyone.

She'd been staring in the direction of Mr. and Mrs. Burns, but not really seeing them, and was surprised to see Mrs. Burns sniff and wipe her eyes.

A new possibility flashed into her mind. Women could kill as well as men, although not usually with a knife. From what she'd read, women were more likely to use poison; and they usually killed husbands who deserved to be killed, or children they did not want. Was it possible that Mrs. Burns had murdered O'Halloran? Her husband was upset with O'Halloran about something. Could it be something that involved both of them?

Mrs. Burns interrupted her thoughts, struggling shakily to her feet.

"Do you think we should prepare the evening meal? It's getting late."

"Sergeant Frank said no one was to move until he came back," said Hemi, raising his gun in her direction.

Mette put her hand on the barrel of the gun and pushed it down. "Hemi, keep the gun aimed away from people. We don't want you to kill someone accidentally. Mrs. Burns isn't going to attack you." She saw his chin come out and was sorry she'd spoken. But he dropped the gun slightly without looking at her.

"I think we'd better wait until Frank returns," she said to both of them. "He won't be long."

Mrs. Burns smiled at Hemi. "You were right to point the gun at me. You were given orders and you have to follow them. You're a soldier. Sergeant Hardy is lucky to have you."

Hemi's face lightened, but he said nothing. Now he too was seeing himself as a soldier.

They were sitting still and staring at each other in silence when Frank and Niall appeared through the small stand of trees that stood between the camp and the fence that bordered the O'Halloran farm. Niall's face was white.

"The house has gone," Frank said. "Swept away by the floodwaters."

Arthur tossed an apple core in the fire. "It's starting to run through your house, as well. I was just down there getting apples for Mrs. Hardy. Your parlour is full of eels."

"Eels!" Mette shuddered. To think of her beautiful parlour

full of those beasts. She'd never feel comfortable in that room again.

"I think the water's near its peak," said Frank. "By tomorrow it should start to subside. Then we'll have to think about what we're going to do."

"I could go for help," said Hemi. "I could ride Copenhagen into Feilding - I'd go along the ridge and through the bush until I could see the town, and then work my way downhill until I found someone."

Frank stroked his beard, considering the idea. "I'd been thinking of suggesting that," he said finally. "But it might be difficult for you to get anyone's attention. I'd rather send an adult."

She could tell Frank was also thinking that the Feilding police might not take Hemi seriously because he was a Maori, and was glad that he hadn't said so. But Hemi's expression darkened anyway. "Why not send him to the Pa near Himatangi?" she said, knowing it was too far to the Pa but wanting him to hear a plan that played to his strengths. "He'd have no problem getting the men there to come to our rescue. They could bring their wakas." She saw that Arthur looked puzzled, and explained, "The Pa is the Maori village, and a waka is a dugout canoe."

"I could go to the Pa," said Arthur. "Just tell me the way. Do they speak English there?"

"Too far," said Frank. "And we don't need rescuing. We need to alert the police. Feilding's much closer to us than Himatangi. Five miles compared to twenty. I'm inclined to send someone in to Feilding, as Hemi suggested." He turned to Arthur. "You can ride, can you? I don't want to send anyone who isn't completely comfortable in the saddle."

Especially not on Frank's horse, Mette thought. She'd met

Frank and his horse, Copenhagen, at the same time, and she'd had a special fondness for Copenhagen ever since. She knew the relationship between them

Arthur shrugged. "I rode a bit in Australia. I was down in Botany Bay for years, then I went up to Port Arthur. Not much riding there, but there was in the Bay. For some of us, at least."

Frank frowned. "Botany Bay? You were a convict?"

Arthur sighed. "Got sent out on the last ship in '68 - second to last I think. I was sentenced to three years for stealing a loaf of bread from a bakery to feed my elderly parents, and after a couple of years I got my ticket-of-leave. Once I had my ticket I was given work as a scrim, doing clerical work. They would send me out with letters to the officers' homes. So I'm accustomed to riding hard. Not on a decent horse, either. They gave us old nags to ride. I'd have no trouble with your horse."

"I can't send you until tomorrow," said Frank. "Let me think about it over night. Right now I need some sleep. Hemi, you're going to stand guard for a couple of hours. Then I'll get up and keep watch for the rest of the night."

"I could keep watch," said Arthur. "I…"

Frank shook his head. "No. Sorry Arthur, but Hemi is the only person here I'd trust with my life - other than my wife, of course. And I'm not letting her stay up and keep watch."

* * *

After they'd eaten a meal of cold mutton, hard-boiled eggs, damper and potatoes baked in the ashes, they went to their tents to try to sleep. Frank had put up a canvas lean-to for Arthur near the horses, with instructions for him to keep an eye on them. Arthur was happy to do anything that involved lying down and keeping half an eye on things. She hoped Frank wouldn't send him off on Copenhagen. They'd never see either of them again.

The boys huddled in blankets around the fire, Hemi sitting on a wooden box with the gun across his knees and a pile of wood beside him to keep the fire going. Mette was pleased he was enjoying his task. When everything returned to normal she would suggest to Frank that Hemi needed to be treated as a man now, and to be given more responsibility. Frank had originally taken him on to learn the care of horses, as an unpaid stable boy, at the same time as they had adopted his younger brother, Joey. Perhaps his brother's adoption had made his position more difficult for him, causing him to become the surly young man he had been lately.

"Keep a sharp eye on things," Frank said to Hemi as he followed Mette into their tent. "I'll wake up in two hours. I just need a short kip, then I'll take over from you."

Mette had spread canvas on the ground, and covered it with a layer of towels. They lay down, with Mette's head on Frank's shoulder, and covered themselves with a blanket.

"Not very comfortable for you, is it?" he asked.

"I haven't been comfortable for weeks, even on our nice spring mattress," she said. "But at least it isn't cold. I like sleeping out of doors in this mild weather."

Every night for the past two weeks she'd experienced cramping when she first lay down, and this night was no different. As soon as her head touched Frank's shoulder, her belly tightened up until it felt like a rock. If she lay still and rubbed herself, it eventually softened. In some ways it was a pleasant sensation and she hoped it would be the same when she went into labour. However, her sister Maren had told her that she would know when she was in labour and that the cramps she'd been experiencing were not to be compared with the agony of childbirth. Of course, Maren was prone to exaggeration.

She hadn't told Frank about the cramps, and as far as she could tell he hadn't noticed. She wondered how he'd react when she went into labour. He'd seen plenty of death, but no births that he'd mentioned. He hadn't met his only son until the son was a man. One of these days she'd have to insist that he contact that son.

She heard him start to snore softly and kissed him on the chest, wondering if it was being near him that brought on the cramping, or the fact that she'd changed position.

She was dreaming about her own mother - a wonderful dream that involved rolling the dough for apple cake - when she thought she heard someone say her name. She opened her eyes and lay still. The tent was completely dark and she could barely see the flap. Was she imagining it? Had her mother said her name as part of the dream? She lay listening, scarcely daring to breathe. Was there a murderer outside the tent, calling her to her death? After a few minutes, she heard her name again. This time it was real, not her mother in a dream.

"Mette!"

She tightened her hand on Frank's arm and asked, her voice quavering, "Who's there?"

"It's Hemi. Is Frank going to wake up soon? I've been here for hours…"

She raised herself and shook Frank by the shoulder. "Frank. Wake up."

He sat up, awake instantly.

"Hemi's wondering when you're going to relieve him."

He pulled out his pocket watch and scraped a match against the canvas. The tent lit up like a ghostly ship afloat on a cloud.

"Hell's teeth. I've been asleep for almost four hours. Hemi must be exhausted."

He crawled through the flaps and she heard him apologizing to Hemi.

As she lay back down she had another cramp. The change of position had caused it, not Frank's warm shoulder. She was disappointed. She'd liked the thought that being near him had that effect on her body. She'd had a cramp the last two times they'd been intimate. He hadn't noticed those times either. Men were so unobservant.

She lay there, unable to go back to sleep, listening to Frank and Hemi talking quietly. If this horrible murder brought the two of them together, that would at least mean something good had come from it.

Frank asked Hemi if he knew anything about the ivory-handled carving knife; and Hemi answered that Mette had shown the boys the set of knives last night.

She thought about it. The knife was important. The killer would have to know of its existence. Not Hemi or Joey, of course. Niall? She hoped not. Of course, Mr. Burns had used one of the set to cut up the eels. She'd better tell Frank about that.

She started to drift off, hoping vaguely that she would fall into the same dream she'd been having when Hemi woke her. But an idea jolted her awake. Frank had told her what Niall had said about the goings on at the O'Halloran house. Niall said he'd heard his father doing bad things in the night to his stepmother because he heard his stepmother crying out. But perhaps she was crying out for other reasons that Niall wasn't old enough to understand. Or was he? She remembered when she used to listen to her sister Maren and her husband next door, and how she'd felt about it. Perhaps Niall had developed feelings for his stepmother after listening to them through the wall. Perhaps he had acted on them somehow?

Did his stepmother really climb out the window and escape? They only had Niall's word for that. Perhaps she was somewhere on the property, watching them even now. Perhaps she was a wronged woman - wronged by both father and son - and had come to seek her revenge.

Mette pulled the blanket back over herself and considered the possibility that Sarah O'Halloran had killed her husband, either by herself, or with Niall's help. Did she really run away to town, or had she hidden somewhere, and taken revenge on a husband she hated? She fell asleep with the image of an enraged woman with a knife, coming up to the hill from her farm, ready to kill her husband as he milked the cows. But if that was the case, where was she now? And would she kill again? Were they all in danger from this insane person?

8

The Bush Closes In

Frank squatted beside Hemi, took out his revolver and cocked the hammer. It was new - a Colt Single Action - and he hadn't had a chance to try it out. He'd slipped a box of cartridges in his coat pocket before leading the party up to the paddock, and he took it out now and filled the five empty chambers. He always kept one cartridge chambered when he had his gun on him. Hemi watched, interested, his arms folded against his chest to keep warm, even though it wasn't really cold.

"Can you shoot without stopping with that gun?"

"I have to pull the hammer back - see? Like this. That moves the chamber around to the next cartridge. Then I pull the trigger. But as long as I do both those action, I can keep shooting. It's pretty quick. And I can do it with one hand, or two if I fan it like this."

"Could I try? Not now, but tomorrow when everyone's awake?"

"Sorry, Hemi. I need to keep it close until we find out what happened to Mr. O'Halloran."

"Are you scared?"

Frank looked out into the blackness that surrounded the tents and the fire. "Not scared. But uneasy. We don't know what's out there. Or who."

"Don't you think it must have been Mr. Burns who did it?"

Frank stuffed the empty cartridge box into his coat pocket. "Mr. Burns? Why do you say that?"

"Well, he doesn't like Mr. O'Halloran. And there isn't anyone else. Just Arthur. It couldn't be him. He can't think for himself. Mette had to ask him to get apples, because he was sitting around doing nothing. And he was gone for a long time."

Frank stared at Hemi thoughtfully, remembering himself at Hemi's age. At fifteen he'd been training at Aldershot, and within months he'd been sent to Crimea. Hemi's own father had died fighting with the rebels against the colonial forces, and his aunt was suspected of working with the rebels as well. Fighting was in his blood. Hemi was old enough to start acting and thinking like a man.

"I've been wondering if it could be O'Halloran's wife," he said. "There's no proof that she left. If she didn't, she'll be marooned with us and she may not be thinking straight. We'd better go down to the house at first light and pick up some more ammunition. I should have my rifle with me as well. I didn't think I'd need it, but it looks as if I might."

"Could I have it?" asked Hemi. "I'm a good shooter. Remember how I shot at that lady who was trying to kill you? You can't carry both guns."

Frank put his hand on Hemi's shoulder. "You know, Hemi, I might just let you carry the Enfield. Then I could give your rabbit gun to Arthur if I send him into town. I can't see how I can send anyone else."

"I don't like him," said Hemi. "He's too nosy."

69

"I hadn't noticed. Seems alright to me. Hemi, what do you think of Niall?"

Hemi stared at Frank, shocked. "Niall? You think Niall might have killed his own father?"

"He had reason to do it. Maybe with his stepmother. Did he say anything to you about his family situation?"

"He said he had a stepmother. Sort of like I do, with Mette." Hemi was looking at the ground when he spoke. It was the first time he'd indicated that he might think of Frank and Mette as his parents, in spite of his protestations to the contrary.

Frank decided to keep it simple. "Did he like her?"

Hemi shrugged. "Dunno. That's not something we'd talk about. But he was sorry for her. His mother died years ago, and a couple of years ago his father sent for a new wife. Is that normal? Do people sometimes send away for a wife? I thought you'd have to see someone before you wanted to marry them."

"I'd certainly prefer to see a woman before I married her. But there are more men than women in New Zealand and some men have to take what they can get."

"You were lucky with Mette," said Hemi. "She's nice. Everyone likes her."

"I was very lucky." Frank tried not to smile. "But what about Niall's stepmother? Did he think she was nice? Did he envy his father?"

"I don't think so," said Hemi. "He said his father said she was plain, but at least she was strong and could work on the farm and give him some more children."

Not much of a life for the poor woman. Indentured labour and forced sex.

"Hemi, you'd better get some sleep, but before you do I'm going to check the area to make sure everyone's where they should be and there's no one lurking out there."

Hemi sat up, his gun across his knees, trying - unsuccessfully - not to show his fear. It apparently hadn't occurred to him that someone could be watching them from the surrounding darkness.

Frank circled the camp at the edge of the light, looking inward. The three boys were around the fire, and Arthur was asleep near the horses, curled up under his piece of canvas. He listened outside the Burnses' tent and heard the sound of two people breathing. He lifted the flap to his own tent and saw Mette tangled up in the blankets, looking uncomfortable. He wished he could crawl in beside her.

He took a few minutes to accustom his eyes to the darkness, and then circled the camp again, this time looking outward. The bush was still, broken by the melancholy cry of the morepork, a small brown owl that the Maori considered a guardian. Once when he'd been sent into a rebel encampment on a forward skirmish he'd been told to listen to the sound of the bird. If the cry changed to a shriek, they said, trouble was at hand.

He was almost back to where he'd started when he heard a rustling, followed by the shriek of a morepork. Just a single scream, then complete silence, as if all the night creatures were cowering in the undergrowth, terrified of an intruder. He pulled back the hammer of his revolver, raised it to eye level and stepped carefully in the direction of the sound, knees bent, moving his weapon from side to side. After two or three minutes he stopped and listened. Was that someone panting? He held his own breath and waited. Nothing moved. Had he imagined the panting? He picked up a pine cone, and lobbed it ten feet to his left. Something shuffled in the undergrowth, then stopped. It had almost sounded like scratching. If it was Sarah, perhaps the mosquitoes in the bush had driven her mad. He was used to mosquitoes himself. He found if he ignored them they left him alone.

"I know you're there," he said quietly. "If it's you, Sarah, come out. I know he made your life hell. You might have to go to gaol, but not for long. The courts aren't hard on women in your situation. Best to turn yourself in."

He heard a cough, then someone - or something - started running away from him through the bush. A wild pig? He didn't think so. Not loud enough. And there were no deer in this area, or any other large animals. He followed as best he could, dodging branches in the darkness. The moon came out from between the clouds and cast weird, flickering shadows in the bush. It was almost as if he was at a ball, with dancers swirling around him.

When he reached the creek he came upon a large black dog, its fur full of burrs, crouching in a defensive pose with its back to the water, hackles raised, teeth bared, growling at him. He watched it, his gun raised, trying to assess how tame it was. He'd heard reports recently of feral dogs bothering sheep, but this one didn't look feral. It just looked vicious. Had it been alone, or with other dogs? Could it belong to someone who had brought it here? As he watched, it turned and leapt onto a rock in the middle of the creek and then across to the other side, disappearing into the darkness.

He spent the rest of the night with his senses on high alert, wary of every noise, sure he heard twigs snapping or someone creeping through the undergrowth. Several times, he circled the camp looking out into the darkness. But the dog did not return, and by morning he assumed it had gone on its way. Even in the daylight, however, he still felt the presence of someone, and wondered if Sarah O'Halloran was in the bush, watching them.

* * *

Hemi woke first, keen to do his turn on guard duty, but Frank was having second thoughts. If someone came at them, would Hemi have the fortitude to shoot at the attacker? To shoot a woman, perhaps? Frank doubted that he would. He would have to stay awake until he found out what was going on. He could manage a couple of days without sleep. He had in the past.

He took Joey and Niall down to the house, worried about leaving Mette with a possible killer. He left her seated outside the tent with Hemi beside her, Hemi clutching his rabbit gun. It was the best he could do.

The house looked normal from outside, doors and windows intact, but a line of mud caked around the base of the house showed where the creek had risen. It had retreated now, but the yard was almost impassable; they crossed to the door with difficulty, their boots sticking in the mud with every step. The boot scraper at the front door was completely covered, and Frank thought briefly of Mette, with her insistence that visitors to scrape their boots before they came into her spotless house. All that was now pointless.

The inside of the house looked much like the yard, although there was no sign of the eels Arthur had mentioned. He waded across the parlour to the kitchen and checked the drawer. Only one of the knives was missing - the largest.

The door to the bedroom was ajar, held in place by the mud. Mette had raised her precious spring mattress and balanced it on the bed to keep it away from the floodwaters. It looked dry and safe for now. He eased around the edge of the bed and unlocked the cabinet door, making sure Niall could see what he was doing. "Did your father have a gun, Niall?"

"He had a rifle he kept in the house -in the bedroom, like you, but on the wall. I suppose it's gone now, with the house."

"On the wall? He didn't lock it up then?" One more thing to worry about. A crazed woman roaming around with a rifle.

"No. He said he needed to be able to grab it quickly if someone tried to rob us."

"He wasn't worried about that person getting to it and using it against him?"

Niall looked downcast. "Well, he didn't know someone was going to try and kill him, did he? He had it mostly to kill wild pigs or those dogs that bother the cows and sheep sometimes."

"What kind of gun was it?"

"I don't know." Niall peered at Frank's gun. "Like yours I think. He never let me touch…"

They were interrupted by a high-pitched scream from Joey. "What the hell…where is he?"

"He went to the library to get more books. He said he'd read the ones he took with him."

Frank pushed past Niall and went into the library. Joey was standing on the horse hair couch, his boots leaving a trail of mud across the cushions. Below him a large eel flopped in the mud.

"For god sakes, Joey." Frank took out his knife and strode across to the eel. "It's just an eel. It won't kill you." He plunged

74

his knife into the gill area and hoisted the eel up to show Joey. "See? Dead. Now, I'm going to throw it out the front door."

Joey had grabbed hold of the top shelf in an effort to get himself further away, and had a foothold on a lower shelf. He looked away from Frank nervously. 'I'm going to look for more books."

Frank ignored him and opened the door. He twisted the knife one more time into the eel, noticing that it hadn't quite been dead, and tossed it into the yard.

"Alright then. Get down from there. And buck up, Joey. We all need to be brave now. We can't afford to have anyone…"

"I found something." Joey pulled a small parcel wrapped in brown paper down from the top shelf. "It has my name on it."

Frank took the parcel from him, and confirmed that it did have Joey Hardy written on it in Mette's neat writing. He handed it back to Joey. He knew what it was. "It was supposed to be a surprise," he said. "Mette got you some books for Christmas."

"Can I open them now?"

Frank sighed. Mette would not be happy, but if he said no he'd never hear the last of it. "Open it up, take a quick look, then put it back where you found it. And don't tell Mette."

Joey tore eagerly at the paper, ruining any chance that he could hide his discovery from Mette. He grinned at Frank. "She got me two books." He turned them over in his hands. He would be expecting some sort of sensational adventure and was going to be disappointed. And sure enough, Joey's face fell when he saw the covers.

"Lamb's Tales from Shakespeare," he said. "Is it about sheep?"

Frank wasn't sure what the book was about - but not sheep. "I don't think so. I think it's about…Shakespeare. He was a famous writer hundreds of years ago."

"Oh. I expect I'll like it. And this one is called *Heroic Women in British History.* That might be interesting." Joey flipped through the pages. "Do you know these people? Boadicea. Flora MacDonald. Florence Nightingale. Queen Victoria."

"I know the last two," said Frank. "I met Florence Nightingale in Scutari, at the hospital, when I took one of my men there to have his leg removed. The Lady with the Lamp, they called her." He could see Joey was not interested in someone who was famous for carrying a lamp, and added, "Of course, everyone knows Queen Victoria. Why does the book say was she heroic, other than because she had to put up with Prince Albert?"

"It says she…" Joey squinted at the page. "Survived? She's survived eight assassination attempts. Ooh, that sounds more exciting."

"Eight? I had no idea. Put the books back where you found them, Joey. We'd better get going."

"My dad saved her life one time," said Niall. "He was a palace guard."

Frank nodded. He had stories like that too. There was usually a kernel of truth to them. He'd probably been in the barracks when it happened and had claimed heroism ever since.

Joey flicked through the pages again. "There's a man here who looks like Arthur," he said. He held up the book to Frank.

"It does, somewhat," said Frank. "But it's just a drawing. Put it back, Joey. I have one more thing to do and then we'll be off."

He went back into the parlour and checked his drink cabinet - or what he thought of as his drink cabinet, although he had just the one bottle in it. He'd decided to take the whisky with him. It might prove useful if anyone got injured. He remembered

Miss Nightingale making good use of alcohol in the hospital in Scutari when the chloroform ran out.

The bottle felt light. He held it up to the light. Almost gone. Strange. He could have sworn it was close to full when he gave O'Halloran a drink last night. Someone had been in his house, drinking his whisky. Arthur probably, which would explain his relaxed demeanour when he came back with the apples. And also why he felt the need to eat all the apples. He was using them to disguise the smell of alcohol on his breath.

He felt an overwhelming desire to toss down the last of whisky, but resisted. You never knew when you would need a stiff drink. Best to save it for more desperate times.

9

The State of Grace

Mette opened an earthenware pot of salted runner beans and shook the salt off them. The pot contained the last of the beans from her garden that she'd laid down for the winter. Served with a piece of bacon, some potatoes and the remaining bread, they would do for their midday meal.

She could feel Grace Burns watching from the doorway of her tent, where she was huddled with her head on her knees. She'd been staring at the ground earlier.

"Do you have any more of your mixture, Mette?"

Mette glanced at the tent opening. Grace was propped on one elbow, clutching Mette's precious quilt to her chest, her face pale and drawn. Mr. Burns and Arthur had gone to find more wood for kindling, with Hemi covering them with his gun. She wasn't sure Frank would approve of them leaving like that, but she needed kindling for the fire, and it seemed reasonable to say yes when Mr. Burns offered to help.

"I'm sorry, Grace, but my mixture is gone," she lied. She didn't want to waste the last little portion just so Mrs. Burns could have a nice rest. They were all tired. And what if her own cramps got worse? She had been saving the last dose in case they did. "I have some manuka honey, though. You could try that. I've been told it has healing powers. The Maori think so at least."

"Could you mix it with a tiny bit of brandy, do you think? Only, my shakes will start again if I don't have something soon."

"Frank doesn't have any," said Mette, shocked that a woman like Grace Burns, married to a temperance leader, might want brandy.

"He has some whisky, doesn't he?" said Grace. "My husband said he saw him drinking a glass with Mr. O'Halloran last night. I could manage a little glass of whisky with honey mixed in, if that's possible."

Unable to tell a lie, Mette nodded. "He has some at the house. I'll send one of the boys to fetch it when Frank returns. Are you not able to overcome the shaking any other way? Would a cup of tea help?"

Mrs. Burns sighed deeply. "I was hoping to take something - something stronger - while my husband was away from camp. Jeremiah is firmly against spirits. He spends his time travelling around the country lecturing on the ills of alcohol. He's a Good Templar and he speaks at churches and halls. He's very popular and well-paid for his efforts."

"And he leaves you at home?"

"He was away from home when…" She stopped and wiped away a tear. "When…"

"When your little girl died? How awful for you."

Grace Burns stared at the ground, her shoulders shaking. Mette couldn't tell if it was grief making her shake, or something else. "It was dreadful. I don't know how I managed. Darling Jane was unwell - teething and feverish when I put her to bed. I thought a good sleep would make her better. Then in the morning when I went to fetch her for breakfast, she'd gone. She looked so peaceful and beautiful lying there; I couldn't believe she'd left us."

Mette moved closer to Grace Burns and put her arm around her shoulder. Grace leaned on her and started to sniffle. "You're so kind, Mette. You make me feel better. But I wish…"

"Now that I think of it, I may have a tiny bit left," said Mette. "I'll check in the supply tent in a minute." Now she had Grace talking, perhaps she could find out more about the Burnses - see if she could discern any reason for them to kill James O'Halloran. It felt heartless, but Frank would want her to find out as much as she could. She would ask about friends, and if the O'Hallorans weren't among them she would find a reason to ask about them. She stroked Grace's hair gently, and asked, "Did you have any family or friends nearby? Anyone you could ask for help?"

"Most of our friends live north of Bulls. You know Sir William Fox, I imagine, the member of parliament for this area? He's also a leader in the temperance movement, and we visited him several times at Westoe, his estate. He introduced me to Edith Halcombe, the artist who is married to Sir Arthur Halcombe, who…" She stopped as a shudder ran through her body. "Oh dear, I…could you…"

Mette wasn't interested in the social lives of the Burnses. She wanted to know why they didn't like Mr. O'Halloran, not that they socialized with the local gentry. Feeling guilty about withholding her mixture, she asked, "Did Mrs. Halcombe help you when your little girl died? Or did someone else, perhaps?"

"Edith came to visit me when I was in…" Mrs. Burns stopped abruptly and bit her lip, as if she had been going to say something, but had changed her mind.

An idea that had been lurking in the back of Mette's mind rose to the surface. As gently as she could, she asked, "Were you in hospital after your daughter died?"

Mrs. Burns nodded imperceptibly, glancing briefly at Mette and then averting her eye. They both understood it was not a hospital they were talking about. She'd been in the lunatic asylum, Mette was sure of it. That was why she was so happy to see the rain yesterday, and why she had said it was so long since she'd been out in the rain. She had lost her mind when the child died, been sent to an asylum for a time, and still needed laudanum to keep the horrors away.

Mette did not know what to say. How could you ask someone what it was like to spend time in a lunatic asylum? Everyone knew how awful the asylums were. She would have been sent to Mount View, the overcrowded and dangerous asylum in Wellington, the nearest one to their farm in Himatangi. How long had she been there? Did Mr. Burns continue his lecture tours when his wife was in the asylum? There was so much to know, but she was afraid to ask. For now, she would let Grace rest and ask her more questions when she'd had some sleep.

"I'll get my mixture now," she said. "And perhaps you can lie down in your tent. I'm sorry for asking so many questions."

Grace Burns wiped her eyes. Mette could see her hand shaking. She jumped up and went into the supply tent, pretending to search for the mixture she'd already found in her herb basket. After a few minutes, she came out again holding a tea cup with the honey and willow bark powder.

"I found some," she said. "Isn't that lucky? I was sure it was all gone, but then I remembered there was a little scraping..."

Grace Burns reached for the cup, not interested in Mette's excuses. "Oh, thank you, Mette." She dipped her fingers into the cup, scooped up the honey mixture, and spooned it into her mouth, her eyes closed in what looked like ecstasy. She licked her lips, then ran a finger around the bottom of the cup scraping up every last speck of the mixture. When she'd finished she sighed and smiled at Mette. "I feel better already. Thank you so much. I think I'll go and lie down now."

For the next hour, Mette busied herself in the supply tent, organizing the remaining food. She estimated there was enough to feed everyone for three more days, after which they would be limited to eating whatever they could find in the woods. She would send the boys to find morepork eggs, or even huhu grubs if they were desperate, and there would be plenty of milk from Mr. O'Halloran's herd. She could live on milk for a week; perhaps if the O'Halloran's had a butter churn she could make butter. She had learned how to make damper in an open fire with the flour. Of course, there was always the eel, but she had no intention of trying that. The very thought of eating a piece of one of those monsters turned her stomach.

She heard Mr. Burns and the boys returning from the bush and crawled out of the tent. She could see Mr. Burns walking in the direction of the camp, clutching a pile of sticks. Hemi was behind him, the rabbit gun hanging from his shoulder, carrying a smaller load of sticks. He looked pleased with himself. She wondered what Frank would think if he saw that Hemi was not paying attention to his guard duties.

As she thought about him, Frank came over the rise from their house with Joey and Niall. He had his Enfield rifle slung over his shoulder and waved at Mette. Too late for her to ask Mrs. Burns anything more, but she had one important piece of information. She just had no idea how that information would connect to Mr. O'Halloran. Perhaps Grace was embarrassed that she'd been in an asylum, and Mr. O'Halloran had threatened to tell people. It wasn't much of a reason to kill someone. But it was easier to believe than Niall killing his own father.

Joey ran ahead of Frank and Niall, grinning and waving something in one hand - a book, she thought. He was half way between Mr. Burns and Hemi, and Frank, still running towards her, when time slowed down.

First, she heard Frank yell at Joey to stop. Joey spun around and stared at Frank, the emotion draining from his face. She followed his gaze, and turned slowly back to Frank. He had the rifle in his hands, and was plunging the rod into it, ramming the cartridge into place. As she struggled to her feet, she heard Grace Burns come out of the tent and scream. Frank had dropped to one knee and was aiming his rifle at Mr. Burns, one eye closed as he sighted his target. He yelled at Joey again to get down. Her heart pounding, she turned to look at Mr. Burns, who had his arms raised as if in surrender. Hemi was aiming his gun at Mr. Burns, unsure of what to do but following Frank's lead.

His eyes fixed on Frank, Joey finally dropped to the ground, his hands over his ears, huddled with his knees to his chin. Mette could feel his terror.

She saw a puff of smoke as Frank fired, and then the sound hit her ears and echoed around the paddock, bouncing back from the bush. He threw the rifle to the ground, stood, and pulled out his revolver, holding it steady but not firing. Grace Burns screamed again, and began to run in her husband's direction.

But Mr. Burns was still on his feet, his arms sinking slowly to his side, looking around wildly. He had dropped his pile of kindling. Why was he still standing? Had Frank missed? That was impossible. He never missed with his rifle. If he had, why wasn't he shooting again with his revolver?

Mr. Burns took a few stumbling steps away from Hemi, stopped, turned back to Frank and yelled. "You got him."

"Got him?" Mette started to run, feeling heavy and off balance. She had seen without really understanding - a monstrous black shape erupting from the woods in Joey's direction, teeth bared, body extended, and then catapulting to the ground as it was hit by the force of the rifle shot. Now Joey was on his feet, running to her. They met half way as he threw himself into her arms, sobbing. "Sergeant Frank tried to kill me."

"It's alright Joey. It's alright." She stroked his head and hugged him tightly. "He wasn't shooting at you. There was a wild dog coming for you. But Frank shot him."

He pushed away from her, breathing heavily. "A dog?"

She took his hand and dragged him over to where Frank stood, beside Mr. Burns, his revolver at his side.

The body of the dog lay near the edge of the bush that made a barrier between the campsite and the creek. The shot had entered its body through the chest and thrown it backwards.

They converged on the scene, Frank with his revolver raised, moving it around as he searched the area.

"It was coming right at you, Joey," he said. "Didn't you see it?"

Joey was holding Mette's hand in a tight grip. He shook his head, and looked as if he was trying not to cry.

"You scared him, Frank," she said. "He thought you were

shooting at him."

He frowned. "I didn't have time to give him a long explanation."

"Where did it come from?"

"I think it's been hanging around since last night. I heard something in the bush and went to look. I thought it might be a person, but found this dog. It took off over the creek and I assumed it was gone." He nudged it with his foot. "We're going to have to bury the carcass. It could be rabid. I've never seen a dog go for a human like that. He was after the smallest animal in the herd - that's you, Joey."

He had intended it as a joke, but Joey didn't understand. He sniffed loudly, refusing to look at him. Frank shook his head impatiently.

"He's just a little boy," Mette said softly. "And he's been through so much. Could you not…?"

Frank eyed Joey thoughtfully, then came over and put his arm around Mette's shoulders, and patted Joey awkwardly on the back. "I'm sorry, Joey," he said. "But I didn't want to see you attacked by a vicious dog. What would Mette and I do without you? We need you to be a big brother to our new baby."

"Hemi can be his big brother," he said, his voice muffled. "You don't need me."

Frank raised his eyebrows at Mette. "Of course we need you. Don't be silly. Look, Joey. Could you help Niall and Hemi dig a hole for the dog? There are some shovels inside the supply tent. A bit of work will cheer you up. It works for me."

Mette felt Joey shake his head against her, and she hugged him closer and stroked his head. "Not now, Frank. Joey's going to stay with me."

He looked annoyed, but shrugged.

Hemi had been kneeling beside the dog. He stood up, looking at Frank. "Shouldn't I keep everyone covered with the rabbit gun while they're digging a grave for the dog?"

"I'll do the digging," said Mr. Burns. "I'm stronger than I look. But there's no need to cover me while I'm digging, Hemi. Why don't you put down the gun for a while and help me? And Arthur will help...where is Arthur, by the way? Wasn't he with us, Hemi?"

"He was behind me when we came out of the bush," said Hemi. "I heard him...I think. Someone was following me."

"Must've been the dog," said Frank. "You're lucky it didn't attack you from behind. Look, Burns, you and Hemi dig the hole and Niall and I will go and look for Arthur. There might be another dog and it could have him cornered somewhere. Keep the burial site away from the camp and make sure it's deep. We don't want another animal to dig it up." He patted Joey on the back. "Joey, you help Mette get the meal ready. We'll eat when Niall and I return."

Mette sighed. She appreciated the comfortable strength of Frank's authority. He always knew what to do. And he was trying with the boys. Perhaps when he had a child of his own he would understand. Mr. Burns certainly seemed to have been close to his daughter.

"Do you have any whisky at the house?," she asked. "Mrs. Burns would like something to help with her shakes. I gave her the last of my willow bark mixture, but it won't last long. I was going to ask one of the boys to go down there, but now I'm worried."

He reached inside his coat. "I brought this up with me. It's all I have left. Someone's been at it. I had half a bottle left last night. I think it may have been Arthur. He was down there,

86

wasn't he?"

She shook the bottle. "There's hardly any left. Can I give this to her?"

"Do you have to?" he asked. "For all I know she was the one who drank it. Although she wouldn't know I had any. Must have been Arthur."

"She said her husband told her that you had some. He saw you and Mr. O'Halloran having a drink."

"Damn. Well, give her a small glass. I need to save the rest for emergencies. What if we find Arthur chewed up by a dog? We won't have any way of anaesthetizing him."

And what if I go into labour, Mette thought. Frank was very trusting about there still being two weeks before she was due to give birth. But the way she was feeling today, she was wondering if it would be that long. The Danish women from the clearing had told her that it was a good idea to keep things clean during a birth, and whisky was a good way to clean... whatever it was that needed cleaning. Frank would probably need a sip himself to calm his nerves. Like with her willow bark mixture, it was such a waste to share it with someone with the shakes. She would, of course. She found it so hard to say no to anyone who needed her help.

10

Another Body

Frank grappled his way through the bush to the creek, following the track left by Jeremiah Burns, Arthur and Hemi. About fifty yards in he found a spot where the grass had been trodden down and the remnants of a pile of sticks lay scattered. They'd built the pile as they searched the area, returning to bring more dry sticks. In one corner of the flattened area a narrow, flattened track led to the water.

"Looks like one person peeled off in that direction," he said to Niall, who had followed him in silence. "Has to be Arthur. I wonder why? The wood down there would be damp from the spray and no use for firewood."

They followed the narrow track down to the water. The creek was in full spate, tearing at its banks, tumbling branches, fence posts and telegraph wires into knotted clumps. A sheet of corrugated iron spun slowly past, bumping against overhanging trees. Frank guessed it had come from the roof of his stable. He was already dreading the amount of work he was going to have to do to repair his farm after this damned flood - not to mention the cost.

The broken chassis of a Landau coach - presumably the one belonging to Mr. Burns - had been lifted from where they had been rescued, and smashed its way down from the rise. The two wheels and the under chassis were wedged against the bank on the far side. The body of the carriage must have been borne away downstream. When the water subsided they could probably pull it out and get it back into shape, but it was much too dangerous at the moment. The wainwright in Feilding was going to busy repairing all the carriages and drays when this was over. Lots of people were going to be busy. He'd be hard pressed to get anyone to help him.

He called Arthur's name, and waited for a response. Nothing.

"He might not hear you over the sound of the creek," said Niall. "I don't know if he'd go this way. The bush gets pretty thick down near our place."

"You've been here before, have you?" Frank asked. Even when the creek was no more than a trickle in the middle of a dry spell, the track would be hard to navigate. The O'Hallorans had never been to his house; he'd met James O'Halloran for the first time a couple of weeks ago, when the blacksmith in Feilding had introduced him to his neighbour. He'd gone down to the O'Halloran farm when he heard about the floods coming to offer a safe place for his dairy herd and spoken to him briefly to discuss what they could do, and when.

"I used to come up this way looking for rabbits," said Niall. "You know how my father felt about rabbits. He wanted them all dead. But I never came closer to your place than this. I'd have to take the track beside the paddock to get there, and I didn't want to trespass. My father said I shouldn't."

Frank yelled Arthur's name again and waited. He heard nothing. "Let's go, Niall. We'll head down to your house. Keep an eye open for another dog, and stay away from the water. Walk in front of me."

Niall bridled. "You don't trust me, do you? I didn't kill my father, you know."

Frank caught a branch that Niall had pushed aside. "I'm sorry, Niall. But I can't take any chances. I don't know who killed your father. There aren't many possibilities."

Niall started to walk away, his shoulders slumped, and then turned back to Frank. "Couldn't someone else be on the property? The dog got here somehow."

"I saw it leap across the creek last night," said Frank. "A man couldn't do that."

Niall resumed walking, with Frank following close behind. He found it hard to believe that Niall had killed his father, even though he was the person with the most reason to do so. He was so transparent and likeable. If he was lying, he was doing a bloody good job of it.

They were clambering around the base of a partly submerged willow tree when Frank spotted something white caught in the exposed roots below them. It looked like an article of clothing. "Stop a minute, will you, Niall. I see something in the water I want to check."

Niall squatted down and watched as Frank crawled out along a branch that hung a few inches above the water. It dipped with his weight, but stayed above the torrent. He lay down and wrapped his ams around it, steadying himself. "Looks like a sleeve," he said. "From someone's old shirt, or dress."

Niall stood up, looking anxious. "What colour is it?"

"White, I think. A faded white. Could be old."

Niall waded into the water beside the willow tree. "Sarah was wearing a white dress."

"Niall, stay there. I'll lift up the sleeve and you can tell me if it looks familiar. But for God's sake don't come in any further. I don't want to have to rescue…" The sleeve felt heavy. Something was holding it in place. He gave it a hard tug and it rose from below the branch. With it came a limp, pale arm.

Niall's face went white. "It's Sarah. Oh my God, it's Sarah. She must have come up this way…" He moved deeper into the creek. The water was up past his knees, tearing at his clothing, but he ignored it. Frank jumped off the branch to stop him going further. "Get back. Don't do anything foolish. No point in getting swept away yourself."

Niall tried to push past Frank. "We have to get her out of there. We can't just leave her."

Frank grabbed Niall's wrist and held it. "Get up on the branch and see what you can see on the other side. And hold tight. I'm going under. I'm going to leave my revolver on the bank. Unloaded." He removed the cartridges, and tossed the gun onto the bank. Then, taking a deep breath he plunged under the branch and held himself there. He could see nothing in the murky water, but his hand touched what felt like a shoulder. He grabbed hold of a piece of cloth and pulled. The lower part of the body swayed in the current and bumped against his legs, but the upper body stayed where it was. She was wedged firmly under the roots of the tree. With his lungs near to bursting, he reached higher and touched a face. Long hair had wrapped itself around soft cheeks. It was a woman a least. He rose from the water to find that Niall had gone into the water on the opposite side of the branch, and was groping for the body with his head above water.

He retrieved his gun and put it back in his pocket. Then he leaned across the branch and grabbed Niall by his belt. "Go under if you want. I can feel her there but I can't see her. Try to pull her out by her skirt. I'll hold you."

Niall was under for a long time, and came up gasping for air. "I can't move her."

"I think we'd better wait for the flood to recede and get her out then. We may have to chop down the willow. She'll be safe there in the cold water." She'd be better preserved where she was, he thought, than in the tent with Niall's father.

Niall dragged himself reluctantly to the bank. He took off his shirt and wrung it out. Then he sat on a log, tossed his shirt to the ground in front of himself, leaned his head in his hands and began to cry in loud, gasping sobs.

Frank waited for him to finish.

Eventually he sat back, sniffed and rubbed his eyes with the back of his hand, and said, "I'm sorry. It all suddenly became real to me."

"Don't worry," said Frank, who couldn't remember ever being moved to tears, even when his own brother died. "You've been through a lot. I understand."

"I feel stupid. I haven't cried for years."

"Both parents dying within a day of each other. That must be hard to take." Niall had been calmer than expected when he saw the body of his father. Why had he cried like a baby at the sight of his step-mother? There was more to the story than Niall was telling him.

Niall hunched his shoulders and stared at the ground. "It's just that…just that this is my fault," he said.

"Your fault? You tried to save her."

"I shouldn't have sent her off by herself with a flood on the way. I should have gone with her."

"You did your best."

"I could have taken her to my hideaway - I have one up beside your pasture. A place where you can disappear and no one can find you."

"That would have been a temporary solution. Your father would have found you, surely."

Niall shook his head. "I used to go there when he was mad at me, and he never found me. I'd go back home when he'd had time to calm down. Once I spent a whole day in there."

Frank patted him on his bare shoulder. "You did your best. No use second guessing yourself now. We should…"

Niall interrupted him. "Do you think Arthur might have done this to her? Killed her and thrown her into the water? Why has he run off? And I know Hemi was supposed to be watching them, but he thinks Mr. Burns is the murderer and he would be watching him carefully and not notice what Arthur was doing."

Frank thought for a while before answering. Mette had told him her theory, all her theories, including the one about Arthur being hired by Burns to kill O'Halloran. But Arthur was not the type you would hire if you wanted someone killed. Of course, looks were deceiving. Perhaps Arthur was a cold-blooded assassin disguised as an inept, greedy, layabout.

"I can't think of any reason why he might have. He says he's been in the district for a couple of weeks. On the other hand, both your parents are now dead, and he had an opportunity in both cases. Might he have met your father somewhere recently?"

"We never had any visitors at the house. Didn't Arthur say he met Mr. Burns in Foxton? My father went there sometimes. He must have met Mr. Burns there, at least. So maybe he met Arthur in Foxton as well."

"Did your father go to temperance meetings?"

Niall gave a short laugh. "Not him. He liked his drink too much. And he used to say mean things about the templars. He thought they were hypocrites."

"When was the last time he was in Foxton?"

"I can't remember exactly. It's been a while. He was there to pick up Sarah. She came in by the SS *Stormbird* from Wellington. And he sometimes went to get shipments at the port. I remember one time he had a pair of breeding cows sent down from New Plymouth. But that was weeks ago. Last year he was on a jury, so he went there quite a few times. They were short of people to do jury duty and the judge asked him to take part because of his military background. I remember him complaining about it, because he disagreed with rest of the members of the jury. Typical, really. He always thought he knew better than other people. But that was months ago, not recently."

"What about Mr. Burns? Could he have been on the jury with him? Perhaps they disagreed about the verdict."

"I suppose so. He didn't say much about the trial, but I think it was a murder. My father thought it was, anyway."

They sat in silence for several minutes. Frank could feel steam rising from his clothes in the heat. Eventually, he stood up.

"We'd best move on and look for Arthur. See what he has to say for himself."

Niall had started to pull his shirt on, but stopped before he'd completed the task, one arm suspended at shoulder height. "What about the dog? Sarah was afraid of dogs, especially big ones. If she saw that one she could have easily fallen in the creek trying to escape it."

Frank nodded. "You know, that makes a lot of sense. She was cornered by the dog and jumped in the water or onto a branch to get away from it. And then the current got her and she drowned."

"Poor Sarah," said Niall. "She came all the way from Ireland to marry a man she didn't know, and he turned out to be… well, not a very kind person. And now she's dead." He finished pulling on his shirt and turned away from the creek. "What should we do now?"

Frank had been watching Niall closely. He'd almost decided he couldn't possibly have killed his father, but his strange rush of emotion on finding his stepmother's body, followed by this detachment, bothered him. What exactly had been the relationship between him and Sarah?

"Were you friends, the two of you?" he asked. "You and Sarah?"

Niall blushed. "Friends? Not really. Why would we be friends? She was my step mother."

"Did you sleep with her, Niall?"

Niall's face turned even redder.

"Of course not."

"Your face is telling a different story."

"No, I…well, I didn't mean to. And we didn't really do anything. At least I don't think we did. But she climbed into bed with me that day when my father was in the barn. She said she wanted to cuddle with me, because she missed her mother and she was sad. I didn't know what to do. That's when I told her I would help her escape. I thought things would be easier for me if she was gone. It wasn't just for her that I helped her."

Clearly the boy had mixed feelings about his stepmother. Frank shoved his revolver into his belt and stood up. Time to find Arthur. He would push Niall more another time. Bit by bit he was revealing the whole story.

"Let's go."

They struggled through the bush, climbing over fallen trees and pushing aside vines. Close to the creek like this it was hard to tell where someone might have walked. Everything was damp, and footprints filled in instantly. Frank found what he thought could be a boot print in the mud beside a tree trunk where someone might have climbed over, but it could just as easily been left there by the dog as it was little more than an indentation.

Through the trees he could see what was left of the O'Halloran farmhouse. The walls and roof had gone, but the foundation was still in place, with a few studs standing where the doorway had been. He tried calling again. "Arthur? Are you there?"

He heard a faint sound above the thunder of the water. He thought someone had said, "Down here."

He ran through the last fifty yards of bush. At the edge of the O'Halloran's farm yard, Arthur sat on the stump of a felled tree, his back to them. He turned to them, his face sorrowful. His hat was clutched in both hands and he was twisting it around. "Someone attacked me."

"Did you see who it was?"

Arthur shook his head and then winced. "He hit me on the head. I blacked out for ages."

"Are you cut? Where were you hit?"

"On the back of the head." He rubbed his head. "I don't have a cut, because I was wearing my hat, but it hurts like hell. There's going to be a lump in a day or two."

"My father uses - used to use - extract of eucalyptus for

bruises," said Niall. "It keeps the lumps down."

"On his cows?" asked Arthur doubtfully. "I wouldn't use anything that's used for cows."

"Mette makes a tea of eucalyptus leaves," said Frank. "But not for bruises. For colds and influenza. She'll have some with her at the campsite. Listen, Arthur. Who hit you? Did you see? And where were you when it happened? Down here?"

"Well..." Arthur looked around. "I don't remember exactly. I was heading down this way to see if Mr. O'Halloran had a wood pile, and next thing I knew I found myself sitting here with a sore head."

Frank could not see any sign of a mark on Arthur's head. But putting together the fact that Arthur was extremely lazy, and the fact that O'Halloran could have had some alcohol in his house, he could guess why Arthur had come down this way. He was looking to see what he could scavenge for himself.

Had he encountered Sarah O'Halloran on the way down and fought with her before she drowned? It was unlikely. There hadn't been time for that. It was also unlikely that Arthur had actually been hit on the back of the head. A more likely explanation was that he intended to use his sore head as an excuse to get out of work. Frank had seen men like that in the army - malingerers who got out of any job they could, some even injuring themselves.

"Could you have hit it against a branch?"

"I suppose so," said Arthur. "But it feels like I got hit with a nightstick."

Frank looked more closely at the back of Arthur's head. Not the faintest sign of a nightstick. His hair was barely disturbed. Of course he had been wearing that hat. "Time to get back to camp," he said. "Mette will have a look at your head, Arthur. She'll have a cure of some kind. A mustard plaster or something. And Niall, you'd better see to the herd. I'll send Hemi with you to milk the cows."

Niall's face sagged. "Will he have his gun?"

Frank sighed. "I'm sorry, Niall, but yes he will."

As they returned to the camp site, another possibility occurred to him. What if Sarah O'Halloran had murdered her husband, and then thrown herself into the creek? If that was the case they'd never know for certain. Something would need to surface that made things clearer.

11

Milk and Honey

Mette felt as if they were on a picnic. The sun had come out and a pleasant breeze rippled the grass around the campsite. She spread out blankets and laid out tin plates and cups, the ones they used when they went to the Palmerston Sports Day or the New Year's Races in Feilding. In the centre of the circle of plates she placed plates of bacon and damper, and their last piece of English cheese. Arthur had eaten most of the apples, but she cut the three she had left in quarters, removed the cores, and put them beside the damper. Arthur had gone to rest his aching head in the shade of the blossoming pohutakawa trees near the horses, taking a large slice of damper with him. He'd asked if she had any cheese to eat with it, and she'd been forced to lie. It was amazing how thin he was, considering how much he ate. Her mother used to say someone like that had hollow legs.

Hemi and Niall came back carrying a billy can full of milk each. They had milked all the cows, but discarded most of it as it was impossible for them to drink more than the two billies before it went off in this heat. One billy went into the supply tent for later. The other, Mette put in the shade beside the tent, covering it with a piece of white cambric with stones stitched around the edge so it wouldn't blow away. She didn't want to see mosquitoes or flies floating on top when she drank it. Even with the cambric she always checked the milk before she drank it, just in case.

While they waited for lunch, Hemi and Niall sat in the long grass outside the campsite playing knucklebones. The click click of the game was soothing. They'd invited Joey to join them, but he preferred to read. He was hunched in the shade beside the tent reading one of the books she had planned to give him for Christmas. It was a pity he'd found the gift. Now she'd have to find him something else. Maybe a bag of marbles. She'd already bought some for Hemi.

"Are you enjoying your book, Joey?"

He looked up, his mind still in his book. "What?"

"Don't say what," she said. She'd learned that saying 'what?' was considered rude in English. "Say, pardon me, or I beg your pardon."

"What did you…I mean pardon me, did you say something? That sounds silly, mumma."

She had to agree. After being with Frank for two years, her English was almost perfect but sometimes small differences eluded her.

"I asked you if you were enjoying your book, Joey."

"I like some of the stories," he said. "I like the one about Flora MacDonald rowing Bonnie Prince Charlie, the Pretender, to Skye. Do you know why he was called a Pretender? What was he pretending to do?"

Mette was momentarily distracted. She'd seen Frank coming from the ridge where he'd gone to inspect the property from above. She could see him looking first one way then the other as he walked along the ridge. At the place where he'd built the seat, her favourite place on the whole property, he stopped and jumped down.

"Mumma?"

"What?" she asked, then turned to see Joey smirking at her. He held up the book and pointed to a drawing that accompanied one of the stories. "Did you see this man here that looks like Arthur?"

Mette glanced at it. "I suppose it does. Did he help Flora MacDonald row Bonnie Prince Charlie to Skye?"

"What?"

She started to giggle, and after a minute he joined her. They used to laugh together all the time, but lately he had become so serious and timid they hardly ever shared a joke. She took his hand in hers. "Everything will be back to normal soon, Joey. And then I'll take you into Palmerston and buy you any book you want. That will make you happy, won't it?"

Six months ago, they had been trapped in a burning house with Frank's friend Hop Li, the cook from the Royal Hotel in Palmerston. It was Joey who had accidentally started the fire, and his guilt had gnawed at him ever since.

She left Joey and finished laying out the food. She felt very relaxed, and not the least bit crampy at the moment. Was crampy a word in English? It sounded as if it should be.

Mr. Burns crawled from the tent, where he'd been checking on his wife. They seemed to be perfectly nice people, as did Niall. She felt safe with all of them. In fact, she had decided that it must have been Sarah O'Halloran who killed her husband, and had then thrown herself in the creek. That was the simplest explanation, and also meant they were safe now.

Mr. Burns sat down on the blanket and smiled appreciatively. "You're taking good care of us, Mrs. Hardy. And I can't thank you enough for being so kind to my wife."

"She was telling me a little of what happened," said Mette, watching Mr Burns closely as she spoke.

He examined his nails. "What did she tell you?"

"She told me she was alone when your little girl died. How dreadful that must have been."

He said nothing, but she saw his fists clench. Then he looked up and said, "It was dreadful for me as well."

Mette nodded. "I'm sure it was. How long was she alone before you arrived back at your farm?"

"She wasn't on the farm," said Burns. "Did she tell you that she was?"

Mette thought back to her talk with Grace. "I suppose not. She said you were away from home, but she didn't say where she was. I assumed she was alone in your house with…"

"With her dead child? No. She was in Foxton staying with a friend of ours. The wife of a leader in the temperance movement. He was with me on the lecture tour."

"Not Sir William Fox?"

"No, another…she told you quite a bit, didn't she? She hasn't spoken much about it since it happened. Did you question her about it?"

"I was trying to distract her from wanting more laudanum. I gave her the last of my mixture; I didn't want her to start shaking again."

He turned and looked at the tent, perhaps to make sure his wife heard him. "She has to stop relying on laudanum. I have no idea how to get her off it, but it's ruining our lives."

"Have you tried Holloway's Pills? Some of the Danish women

I know take those. They swear they're effective for calming their nerves."

He frowned "Don't ever take patent medicine, Mrs. Hardy. Much of it is thinly disguised alcohol. All it does is make the manufacturers very wealthy and sell more newspapers. Most tonics that purport to cure alcohol addiction have as much alcohol in them as the real thing."

"I prefer a good walk in the outdoors," said Mette. "I find the fresh air invigorating. Perhaps you should encourage Mrs. Burns to go for long walks."

He nodded. "Perhaps. You're certainly very healthy. Lucky for us that you were there to rescue us. We could have died trying to get to the dispensary in Feilding, but you saved us from the creek."

"I was wondering why you didn't go into Foxton. Isn't that closer to your farm?"

He didn't answer her, but glanced at the ridge.

"Ah, here comes Sergeant Hardy."

She didn't want to finish their discussion yet. Uncertain of what else she could say, she returned to the previous subject. "My sister uses Holloway's Ointment when her children complain of itchy skin, but I…"

He glared at her. It was the first time she'd seen him upset.

"Tell your sister she's a damn fool."

She wasn't going to tell Maren that, but nodded obediently, wondering what it was that had upset him so much.

They sat around the picnic on the blankets and ate in an awkward silence. Grace Burns had awoken and come from her tent. She looked somewhat better, and Mette wondered if giving her something other than the laudanum while she

103

recovered from the shakes was actually a good plan. She would look into that when she was in Palmerston next time. The public library had some excellent medical books and she'd used the last of the money from her pamphlets to buy an annual library subscription. It had cost a pound, and she had not told Frank. He'd said her pamphlet money was hers to spend as she wanted, but knowing how short he was of cash for the farm, she felt guilty. A little guilty.

Joey came out from his lair beside the tent, reading as he walked, and crouched on the rug with his elbows on his knees with the book in front of him.

"You're quite the reader, aren't you, Joey," said Arthur. "I was the same at your age. Couldn't keep me out of the library."

"Where did you live when you were a boy?" asked Mette. She knew so little about Arthur, other than that he had been sent to Botany Bay for trying to help his family, and that he was lazy and greedy.

"I grew up in East London," he said. "In Whitechapel. My parents were Irish, but they moved to London before I was born. I have six brothers and sisters, so it was hard for us growing up. We didn't have much to eat and fought for scraps."

That explained his constant hunger, Mette thought. "Well, you don't have to worry any more now. We may be a little short of food, but we have enough to last us until the flood subsides."

Joey looked up from his book. "Somebody ate my eel."

Arthur slapped him on the shoulder. "I may have taken a little. I didn't know it was yours. Someone should have told me."

"I'm sure Joey doesn't mind, do you Joey?"

Joey went back to reading his book, but Arthur wasn't done

with him. "That looks like an interesting book you have there, Joey."

Joey glanced up at it. "It has a drawing of you in it."

"May I see?"

Joey handed him the book. Arthur flipped through the pages, and then gave it back. "Well that's not very complimentary," he said. "Saying I look like that. I'm hurt."

"I believe Joey has a good eye for faces," said Grace Burns. "Joey, I'd love to teach you how to draw. Do you think you'd like to learn?"

Joey closed his book, keeping his place with one finger. "Could you teach me to draw today?"

Grace Burns laughed. "As soon as we've finished eating," she said. "Unfortunately, I don't have any paper with me, although I saw your mama with a pencil earlier checking off the supplies list."

"You can use the back pages of Joey's book," said Mette. "Joey, give it Grace."

"After lunch," he said. "I'm going to read it now."

Mr. Burns was looking at his wife and frowning. Mette would have expected him to be happy, seeing her improve the way she had.

"This is excellent bacon, Mrs. Hardy," he said. "But I wonder if you have some water or milk. It's quite salty."

She jumped up. "Of course. I'm sorry. I have some milk beside the tent. I was keeping it cool."

She brought out the billy and passed it around to everyone. They all took some except Grace Burns, who gave it to her husband without taking any, saying it would upset her stomach.

"This won't upset your stomach," said Niall, holding up his

cup. "It hasn't been adulterated with water, like you get in towns. It's straight from the cow. The best kind." He balanced his cup on the ground in front of himself and began digging into the food.

Mette eased herself back onto the rug next to Frank, took the billy and started to pour the last cupful for herself. She was surprised to see a lump of something flop into her cup. She poured a little more, saw another lump, and said, "Joey, did you…?"

She touched the lump tentatively and nudged it around the surface of the milk.

Oats. She was looking at oats. Why would someone put oats in the milk?

In a flash of memory, Frank's conversation with Arthur as they walked up to the high paddock on came back to her. Mr. O'Halloran had placed oats boiled in arsenic around his property to kill the rabbits.

She looked around wildly. No one was drinking yet, except Frank, who had the cup at his lips and was tipping it back slowly.

She lunged at him and hit the cup from his hand, feeling her belly contract as she did so. "Frank, Frank…"

He turned to her in alarm, wiping his lips. "What's happening? Are you…?

She could hardly get enough breath to speak. "Someone put poisoned oats in the milk." She dumped the last of the milk in front of him. "Look at this."

He touched the lumpy milk, and then looked around. "No one else drink it. Put your cups down."

Arthur had already lifted the cup to his lips. He threw it down and clutched his stomach. "Oh no. I'm going to die."

"How much did you drink?"

"Just a sip. I feel sick already."

"A sip won't kill you," said Frank. "You're not a rabbit. Spit out as much as you can. And wash everything that might have touched it. Hemi, go and get a bucket of water from the trough. Joey, get some carbolic soap from the supply tent. We should all wash our hands and faces thoroughly. Gargle with the soapy water as well if you tasted the milk. It'll help you vomit."

"What should we do with the poisoned milk?" asked Mr. Burns. He had set his cup in front of him, as far away as possible. "We can't leave it sitting around."

"We could throw it in the creek," suggested Niall. "It will dissipate in the water, and the water's moving so quickly it'll spread out and be harmless."

"Are you sure about that, Niall?" asked Frank. "And come to think of it, where did your father keep the arsenic? Is it still down at your farm?"

"He had a pot he used to boil the arsenic and oats. It was in the barn. The pot would still be there, I think, but not the oats. The barn is on higher ground. Do you think someone got the poison from the barn?"

Frank looked preoccupied. "Could have got them from anywhere around your property," he said. He started walking back and forward, tugging at his beard. Mette could tell he was working something out. Finally, he stood in front of them and glared down at them. "Someone in this group poisoned the milk. It wasn't me or my wife, and I'm sure it wasn't Joey or Hemi. That leaves four of you. Any one of my family could have died. We all could have died. I'm going to damn well find out who did it."

"It wasn't me," said Mr. Burns. "Or my wife."

"Why would I poison anyone?" asked Arthur. "I didn't even know that there was any poison around. If the Burnses didn't do it, and if I didn't do it, that leaves…"

Everyone stared at Niall, who blushed bright red. "Of course I didn't do it. And I didn't kill my father either."

Poor Niall, thought Mette. Now he's reminded everyone that he had the most reason to kill his father, as well as being the person with access to the milk. She wanted to say, no one thinks it was you, Niall. But that would imply she thought it was the Burnses - one of them - who had done it, and she didn't want to point the blame at them while they sat there. She wished she'd had a chance to tell Frank about her talk with Mr. Burns.

"I didn't expect a confession," said Frank. "But, goddamn it, I'm going to tear one out of one of you."

"Frank, could we talk for a few minutes please?"

Frank stared at Mette as if he was trying to read her expression. Then he turned back to the group. "My wife and I are going up to the seat on the ridge to talk. I'll have my guns with me and I'll be watching you. Don't bloody well move an inch. Hemi, Joey, you come with us. Hemi, get your rabbit gun and bring it with you.

Hemi took off to his tent to get his gun. Frank strode up to the seat with Mette behind him doing her best to keep up. They sat with Joey between them. He clung to Mette nervously.

"Now," said Frank. She could see he was angry. "What is it that you want to tell me?"

12

The High Court

Frank was annoyed with Joey, who'd squeezed between them and was leaning on Mette like a child. He wished the two of them were alone without Joey. He was boiling with anger, the rage blocking him from thinking through what had happened, but he could calm himself much more easily if he was alone with Mette. He had his gun resting on his lap, and the rifle propped beside him, ready to bring down anyone at the campsite who made a move. He doubted anyone would try anything. The killer was not yet out in the open. He would drive him out.

"What do you want to tell me?" he asked Mette again. "Do you think you know who's responsible for all this?"

"Mr. and Mrs. Burns aren't telling the truth," she said. "At least Mrs. Burns isn't. And Mr. Burns is angry with his wife about something she did. She told me - or at least she implied - she was at home when her baby died. By herself. But he told me earlier she was in Foxton with friends while he was away on a speaking tour. I know she was in the asylum in Wellington for a while and I assumed she'd broken down when her daughter died. But it's more than that. When I pulled them out of the creek, he said she just wanted to die. She wanted to die, and he wasn't going to let her get away with it again. Again! I wondered at the time what he meant when he said that."

"Sounds like she tried to kill herself," said Frank. "That would be a reason for sending her to the asylum. What's Hemi up to?" He squinted towards the campsite. Hemi had come out of the supply tent where he'd stored his kit, and had hurried off in the direction of the cow pasture.

"He probably left his gun at the pasture," said Joey.

"Damn," said Frank. "He must have. Mette, did you notice if he was carrying it when he came back from milking?"

She closed her eyes and tried to picture the two boys returning from the pasture. "I'm not sure. They were carrying a billy full of milk each. He would have had the gun slung over his shoulder. I remember when he left he was carrying it like that. I think perhaps he wasn't carrying it, but I couldn't swear to it. Do you think he's in danger?"

"He'll be safe as long as no one moves," said Frank. He ran his fingers through his hair and grimaced. "I hope he finds it. We have enough trouble already without a weapon going missing. So, back to the Burnses. What else did they say?"

"Mr. Burns was annoyed that Grace had said anything to me. And upset that she couldn't get off laudanum. I suggested giving her Holloway's Pills instead, and he was irritated about that. He's very much against patent medicine. The first time I mentioned trying the pills he reprimanded me, more or less. But then when I told him Maren uses the cream on her children, he got angry. Angrier than I would have expected. He's mostly quite a self-controlled person."

"I wonder how she tried to kill herself, if she did?" said Frank. "Something to do with a patent medicine? Or did she take an overdose of laudanum? However she did it, he could have had her committed for trying to kill herself. I can see why they're upset with each other, but how would that have anything to do with O'Halloran?"

"Don't you need to go before a coroners' jury to have someone committed?" asked Mette. "Perhaps Mr. O'Halloran was on the jury…"

"Yes. He did jury duty in Foxton." said Frank. "Niall told me his father went into Foxton several times, including a few months ago when he was asked to sit on a jury. And he - Niall - also said his father thought the person was guilty and he was annoyed when he got away with it. He always knew best, that's what Niall said." He scratched his cheek and stretched his body upwards. "You were asleep, but when Arthur first appeared O'Halloran was in the yard in the dark, and he said, 'I know what you did.' I believed he was talking to Niall at first. But perhaps he thought Arthur was Mr. Burns. And Mr. Burns understood something from what he said, and it made him want to kill O'Halloran. He knew something that Burns had done."

"We don't know enough," said Mette. "We need to get Mr. Burns to talk. If he didn't do anything he shouldn't mind telling us about the trial."

"Joey, run down and tell Mr. Burns I want to talk to him," said Frank. He picked Joey up by the armpits and deposited him on the ground beneath the seat. "Don't get too close to the group, and stay off to one side so I can get a clear shot if I need to."

Joey stood there, not moving, staring at Frank anxiously.

"Go, Joey," said Frank. "I can't ask Mette to run down and get him."

Joey took a couple of tentative steps. "You won't shoot me, will you?"

"Not on purpose," said Frank. "Look, Joey, there's no time to argue. Go down there keeping to the left, and stop about twenty feet from the supply tent. Then say in your loudest voice that Sergeant Hardy wants to talk to Mr. Burns if he wouldn't mind coming up here. Pretend you're a staff sergeant."

Joey walked tentatively down the hill, keeping to the left as instructed.

"He's so bloody timid," said Frank. "He didn't used to be like that."

"He has nightmares," said Mette. "You of all people should know about that. And he feels guilty about the fire and what happened to Hop Li. He thinks it's his fault."

Frank sighed. "I know. I'm sorry I'm so tough on him, but pandering to his timidity won't help. He'll do better in life if he's manly and not a craven coward. It won't do him any good in the world to be the way he is now."

He'd moved closer and put his arm around her, making sure he didn't take his eyes off Joey and the people at the camp site. "I can't believe how well you're managing this," he said. "I was wishing I had someone to be my partner in investigating this murder, and here you were all the time." He saw her face go pink with pleasure and gave her a quick kiss on the top of her head. "It will all be over soon. There are only four suspects. We'll soon sort out who did it."

Mr. Burns came up the hill, his face a mixture of emotions:

interest, alarm, even guilt.

"You wanted to see me, Sergeant Hardy?"

They were sitting above him as if they were military judges at a court-martial, which seemed appropriate to Frank. If he had something to tell them, his subordinate position would help force the issue. Joey had crouched down behind Burns, apparently realizing that huddling up to Mette did not look good in this situation.

"We need to know what went on between you and your wife, and why she was in an asylum. Did she try to kill herself?"

Mr. Burns glared at Mette. "My wife told you that too, did she?"

"She didn't say she'd been in an asylum, but I guessed," said Mette. "I asked her if she'd been in hospital. And you hinted that she'd tried to kill herself when I first pulled you from the creek. You said she wouldn't get away with it again."

Burns stood for a long time looking at his feet. Finally he squared his shoulders as if he'd made a decision. He looked up at Frank and said, "She did try to kill herself. After Jane died. She threw herself off the dock early in the morning when the tide was going out. Fortunately, she got stuck on a sandbar, and a fisherman who was setting out to catch schnapper dragged her into his boat and brought her back to Foxton."

"And that was why you had her committed?"

"I didn't have her committed. She was tried for attempted suicide, but the judge decided to send her to the asylum instead of to prison. And some weeks after that, Sir William intervened and had her released into my care."

"Has she attempted to kill herself again?"

He bit his lip and looked Frank in the eye. "I'm not sure. When we were crossing the creek I believe she threw herself out of the carriage, but it may have been that the carriage was already overturning. Arthur grabbed her and she dragged him into the creek. She could have killed him. It's a miracle he survived."

"The asylum must have been a terrible place for someone who'd just lost a daughter," said Mette. "Did you visit her there?"

He nodded. "It was dreadful. Overcrowded and dirty, and full of people who were actually insane. She spent the whole time huddled in a bed, afraid to sleep. I visited her as often as I could; I even moved to Wellington and stayed with a friend. When she came out she was in a terrible state, and insisted I take her to a dispensary right away to get some more laudanum. Foolishly, I agreed."

"She seems to be improving now," said Mette. Frank could see she sympathized with the Burnses. She had an easy face to read. Not to worry. She had softened up Burns for an attack from him.

"Was O'Halloran on the jury?"

"The...the jury?"

"The jury in Foxton where your wife was tried. I know he'd been on a jury in Foxton, about a year ago."

Burns nodded. "Yes. Yes, he was."

"Was that why your were so upset to see him in my parlour?"

Burns nodded again. "The judge was going to send her home with me, but O'Halloran kept insisting she should be sent to gaol. He was the chairman of the jury and the rest of them were afraid to disagree. He was a bully, as I'm sure you noticed. In the end, the judge compromised and sent her to the asylum. The judge told me privately that if I knew anyone powerful I should get that person to put in a word for my wife. And of course I know Sir William Fox well. I hated to ask him for help, but he was very kind. He sent a letter to the governor of the asylum and she was released soon after."

Frank watched him as he spoke. He was obviously upset, but he was not the type to kill someone - if there was such a thing as a type. He and his wife had been through trying times. Maybe it had all been too much for them. Seeing O'Halloran trapped with them by the floodwaters could have pushed him over the edge.

"Could I talk to your wife?"

"Absolutely not. Any questions you have, ask me. I won't have her badgered."

"Perhaps I could talk to Arthur then."

"He knows nothing," said Burns. "I hired him ten days ago. He wasn't around last year, and neither of us has said anything to him."

"Nonetheless," said Frank. "I'd like to get his impressions. Could you return to the camp and send him up?"

Burns spun on his heel and marched down the hill.

"Do you think he's told us everything?" Frank asked Mette.

"I don't know. Oh dear. How horrible it must have been for poor Grace."

"If her husband killed O'Halloran, things are going to get a lot worse for her."

Mette looked at him, shocked. "Sometimes you're so heartless, Frank."

"If everyone gave way to emotion in times like this we'd have killers roaming the countryside," he said shortly. But deep down he knew Mette was right. He'd been away from his own family his entire life, and now that he was building one of his own he was starting to realize that sometimes events had impacts that could not be analyzed in a logical way. The death of his brother had shaken him to the core, but he'd buried it deep in his mind and the memory only surfaced at night when he dreamed about him. And finding he had an illegitimate son had not fazed him either. The son was nothing to him, and yet now he was going to have a son with Mette, and that new son would be just as connected to him as the older one. He felt a small twinge in his gut and a rush of acid in his throat. He'd swallowed soapy water and forced himself to vomit, but apparently some of the poison had already worked its way into his stomach. Something else he didn't need right now.

They sat in silence as Arthur dragged himself up the hill to the seat. He was a slow walker and it took several minutes for him to cover the hundred or so yards.

"Mr. Burns says you have some questions for me?"

"Just a few, about Mr. and Mrs. Burns. Do you have any knowledge of what went on when their child died?"

"Some," he said. "There's a Maori girl comes in and tidies up a couple of times a week. She's told me a couple of things."

"Burns said Mrs. Burns tried to kill herself last year. And then again when you were in the carriage."

"Threw herself into the water," said Arthur. "Jumped right across me to do it. I grabbed her out of instinct, and next thing I knew I was in the water. He got hold of her and left me to it. I was bloody lucky to survive."

"It's natural that he'd try to save his wife first," said Mette. "And I'm sure everything happened so fast…"

Arthur shrugged. "I suppose…what else did you want to ask me?"

"I was wondering if you knew anything about O'Halloran,"

said Frank. He saw Arthur's eyes narrow. He knew something. "You heard about the coroner's jury, and how O'Halloran argued against letting her go free?"

Arthur looked puzzled. "Coroner's jury? What coroners jury?"

"She tried to kill herself in Foxton by throwing herself in the river…"

"I heard about that," said Arthur. "Pania - that was the girl who came in and tidied up - told me she was pulled onto a boat, else her body might have never been found."

"There was a coroners' jury," said Frank. "To see if she should be tried for suicide."

"Was there?" said Arthur. "But there was a trial as well. And it wasn't for her suicide attempt. It was for murder."

Frank and Mette turned to each other, then back at Arthur.

"Murder?" they said together.

"Yeah. She killed her baby. Not on purpose, mind you, but accidentally. It was - what do you call it - infanticide."

Mette clutched her chest. "How was that possible? She told me she put her little girl to bed, and in the morning she was gone. Did they blame her for that?"

"Put her to bed," said Arthur. "But first…well, the baby was having trouble with her teeth coming in, and Mrs. Burns rubbed some laudanum on her gums. They said that was what killed the baby. They said she was responsible for the baby's death. And they tried her for it."

13

The Suspects

Mette tried hard to catch her breath. Grace Burns had rubbed laudanum on Jane's gums, and had killed her daughter? How heartbreaking. No wonder she'd tried to kill herself. How could she live with the guilt?

"Mette, are you alright? You're breathing strangely." Frank looked away from the campsite for the first time since they'd been on the seat and put an arm around her.

She leaned against him, clutched his collar, and started to sniff. "I can't bear it. Grace killed her own little daughter. How can she live with that...I..."

He stroked her head and stared down at the campsite, preoccupied with something. She saw him grimace. Something was bothering him. The lack of sleep, probably. Or all the extra responsibility suddenly pressing on him.

Arthur had gone to rejoin the group, with strict instructions not to say anything to Mr. Burns. She could tell Frank was watching him. Watching them all. At least she could be comforted by the fact that nothing more could happen. Frank would not let anything else happen.

"One of them killed O'Halloran," he said. "We have to work out who had the opportunity and the strength to do it. One of the Burnses, I suspect. I know Mrs. Burns is an unlikely suspect, but we can't rule her out. Lunatics can be very strong…"

Mette wiped her eyes. "She's not a lunatic. She's a woman who accidentally killed her baby, and it's not surprising she's upset."

"Technically she's a lunatic," said Frank. "But never mind. I can understand why you feel sorry for her. Let's not argue about that now. We can talk about the Burnses, but maybe we should discuss everyone in the group, one at a time, and work out who had the means, the motive, and the opportunity for both the stabbing and the attempt to poison us."

"Including Niall and Arthur?"

"Of course. In fact, let's start with them. They're the easiest two. How about Arthur? Not much to say about him, other than that he's a convicted criminal."

"He says for stealing bread to feed his family."

"He says," said Frank. "We only have his word for it. And I wouldn't be surprised if all the Australian convicts claim that they were convicted for trying to help their families."

"He drank some milk. Would he do that if he was the one that poisoned it?"

"So did I," said Frank. "Do you see me worrying about it? A rabbit will die from eating a spoonful of boiled oats. But a man who drinks milk tainted with poisoned oats might not even get sick. Arthur could know that, although I don't know how. Did he have an opportunity to put the poison in the milk?"

"He was sleeping behind the supply tent," said Mette. "He could have slipped some in. Joey, did you hear anyone moving

119

behind you when you were reading by the tent?"

"I don't remember," he said. "I don't hear anything when I'm reading."

"He could have put it in when we were passing it around," said Frank. "In fact, anyone could have done it then. We were partially hidden from each other's view by the flames. The poisoner could have held the billy low and dropped in the oats without anyone seeing."

"He'd have to have some handy," said Mette. "Would Arthur be carrying it around in his pocket waiting to kill us all? Really?"

"You could say that about any of them." Frank stretched and winced as if something was hurting on his side. "Ah, God, I'm getting tired. I need some sleep. Let's talk about the possibility that Arthur murdered Mr. O'Halloran. Do you remember how that morning went? The morning we came up to the campsite."

"I got up and you were gone," said Mette. "I heard you in the yard. Mr. and Mrs. Burns were in the kitchen, dressed and ready for breakfast. Mr. O'Halloran had already gone up to milk the cows. We went outside and Arthur came from the stable. I suppose he could have run up the path already, murdered Mr. O'Halloran, then come back and pretended to wake up."

"He's not looking too good as the perpetrator," said Frank. "The big problem with him is motive. I can't think of any reason for him to kill O'Halloran. Although O'Halloran did say, 'I know what you did' when he was shaking him that first night. At the time I assumed he mistook him for Niall. Perhaps he didn't."

"You'd think he would recognize his son, even in the dark," said Mette. "So he either knew it was Arthur, or he thought it was Mr. Burns. So maybe Mr. Burns…"

"We'll talk about him when we finish with Arthur and Niall. O'Halloran would have had to recognize Arthur in the dark and remember where he'd seen him before," said Frank. "Doesn't seem likely. So what about Niall?"

"I've been thinking about him," said Mette. "He fits perfectly, but I just can't believe it's him. He's such a nice boy. Very ready to help me any time I ask him."

Frank nodded. "I like him," he said. "In fact, when all this is over I think we should take him in. He doesn't have a living parent, and…"

"I'd like that," said Joey, who had been following the discussion intently. "I like Niall, and so does Hemi. He could be our brother."

"Only if he wasn't the one who killed his father." Frank's grin turned into a grimace. "I'm not taking on a murderer, no matter how pleasant he is."

"He could have killed his father when he went up to find him," said Mette. "Although why kill him down near the fence? You'd think he'd do it in the pasture. And he could have picked up some poisoned oats when he was in the pasture, or when you found the body, and put it in the milk later. He also knew about the knife, which the others didn't, although they might have guessed we'd have knives in that drawer. But I still don't believe it was Niall."

"We shouldn't eliminate him just because we like him. In Niall's favour is the question, why would he try to poison all of us? It wouldn't make him look less suspicious. The opposite in fact. He is interested in medicine though. I saw a medical book beside his bed before the house washed away. Maybe he's a heartless killer and wanted to see if he could kill with poisoned oats. He's been living in a pretty difficult household."

"That reminds me," said Mette, whose brain was not working quite as well as she was used to. "What about Sarah? I had her pegged as the main suspect."

Frank gave her a look, raised a finger to his lips, and said, "Joey, hop up onto the ridge and see if you can see Hemi coming."

Joey obeyed him. He had gained confidence since his run down to the campsite to fetch Mr. Burns. Once Frank was sure he was out of earshot, he said quietly, "Sarah O'Halloran is dead."

"Oh no! Another murder?"

"I'm not sure. Niall and I found her body trapped under some roots in the creek. We couldn't get her out, so we left her where she was. I prefer that no one else know about it yet."

"The poor woman. Now I'll imagine her floating in the dark water waiting for someone to come and rescue her. What a terrifying end for her, after she escaped from her dreadful husband." She sighed. "But I suppose that brings Arthur back into the picture. He could have killed her when you were out searching for him."

Frank scratched his ear where a mosquito had just feasted on him. "Possibly. Or he could have done it that first night when he came up the the track by the creek looking for our place. But Niall and I thought it might be the dog. He says she was afraid of dogs. It could have scared her into the water and she drowned. She could even have slipped in the dark and drowned."

"I can see Hemi," said Joey from above them. "He's climbing the ridge from the pasture. He'll be here in a minute."

"Thanks Joey," said Frank. "You have eyes like a hawk."

Joey touched his eyes, puzzled. "That means you can see well," said Mette. "Not that you have big droopy hoods over your eyes."

They exchanged a grin, and he squeezed in beside her, sitting upright this time and not clinging. "Are you going to talk about Mr. Burns now?" he asked. "He did it, I think."

"And why do think Mr. Burns killed Mr. O'Halloran?" said Frank.

Joey pulled a face, thinking. "It has to be either Mr. Burns or Arthur. Niall didn't do it because I like him, and Mrs. Burns is a lady, and she's going to teach me how to draw."

"Excellent reasons," said Frank. "Well, Mette? What about the Burnses?"

"How could one of them have killed O'Halloran without the other realizing they had gone somewhere that morning? And wouldn't you have seen someone come out of the house and walk up the path beside the horse paddock?"

"I was in and out of the stables getting the horses ready. He could have slipped by when I wasn't looking. And his wife spends a lot of time sleeping. I wouldn't count out opportunity for him."

"And as far as poisoning the milk goes, he had as many chances as anyone to do that. They both did."

"And Mrs. Burns didn't take any milk," said Frank. "Maybe she was trying to kill her husband and didn't care if everyone died with him."

"I don't think she would have tried to kill Joey." Mette was uncomfortable talking like this in front of him. "She seems very fond of Joey."

Joey jumped suddenly. "The baby just kicked me. I was leaning against you and I felt a kick."

Both Joey and Frank stared at Mette adoringly, and she laughed. "Your little sister will be chasing you around the yard before you know it."

"Little brother," Frank and Joey said together.

"Joey, perhaps you should find a place to sit further down the slope. Sergeant Frank and I need to talk, and it might be too gruesome for you."

"Alright then. But I want to feel another kick. That was fun."

She took his hand and put it on her belly. "See? She's moving all over the place at the moment. She's been kicking me in the ribs all morning."

"Does it feel strange to have someone inside you?"

She nodded. "Now go and sit down there on that trunk. About half way down."

He complied, and she said to Frank, "I wish I didn't have to talk about it either. But it's helpful, isn't it? So, what about Mr. Burns. Isn't he our lead suspect?"

"I'd say so. His wife accidentally killed their baby and, at some point, she attempted suicide. She was in an asylum and has since become addicted to laudanum. The judge was willing to send her home under the care of her husband. That's fairly typical for women who commit infanticide, if they're come from a good family situation. But O'Halloran talked the jury into recommending she be sent to gaol. The judge compromised and committed her to the asylum instead, knowing they had friends who could get her out of there. But she still spent some time in the worst asylum in the colony."

Mette started weeping again. She hadn't wanted to face it, but when Frank laid it all out like that there was almost no other conclusion. Mr. Burns had killed O'Halloran, and it sounded as if he'd had a good reason.

"He wouldn't have tried to poison us," said Frank. "That part doesn't make sense. I can only conclude that it was a suicide attempt by Mrs. Burns."

"Sergeant Frank. Sergeant Frank."

Hemi had come leaping from above holding a small ammo bag. Frank jumped up to meet him. "What's going on?"

"My rabbit gun is gone. It's been stolen. I found my ammo bag lying near the water trough up at the pasture. The pellets are gone. And I can't find my gun anywhere.

Frank grunted out the worst curse that she'd ever heard him say. She was glad Joey was out of earshot. Then he repeated it and doubled over, groaning.

She eased herself off the seat and leaned over him, clutching his shoulders. "Frank. What is it? What's happening?"

"Poison must have got to my gut," he said through clenched teeth. "Get me back to the campsite. Need to get rid of it." He sank to his knees, still doubled over.

"Hemi, get on the other side," said Mette. "Get his arm over your shoulder and help me get him to the campsite."

They took an arm each and tried to move him.

"He's too big," said Hemi. "We don't have enough leverage."

Frank managed to get up on one knee. "Wait...wait...when I get to my feet, get hold of me," he said. He staggered to his feet for a few seconds and they managed to get themselves in place under his arms.

Joey was waiting for them at his tree stump, his eyes wide with fear, clutching his knees. "Is Sergeant Frank going to die?"

Mette stopped. "I have to take a break. I don't think I can..."

"Mrs Hardy, Mrs. Hardy." Niall had left the campsite and was running towards them. "Let me help."

She moved aside and Niall took her place. Together he and

Hemi manhandled Frank back to the campsite, with the much taller Niall bearing most of the load.

"Is it the poison?" asked Niall as they dropped Frank in front of his tent.

Mette nodded. Her heart was pounding. She had no idea what to do. She had all kinds of cures for childhood diseases, headaches, mosquito bites and constipation. But she had no idea what to do for someone who'd been poisoned with arsenic. What on earth was the antidote? And did they have what they needed in their supplies?

14

A Gut Punch

He didn't have long to live. He was sure of it. The pain was worse than anything he'd felt on the battlefield. He was freezing, his teeth chattering with the cold, while sweat dripped down his cheek, through his beard, pooling on his neck. He couldn't move.

"Dry mustard in water to make him vomit. Then strong, boiled tea with lots of salt, to wash any poison through" someone said. He saw his brother leaning over him anxiously. A big man with dark hair and blue eyes. But his brother had brown eyes like his own. And his brother had died a dozen or more years ago, during the war. Not his brother, then.

"We have some down at the barn already mixed. We give it to the cows if they get into the poison."

"Go get it, Niall."

"Send ... Hemi," he managed to croak.

An angry, "I'll drink some in front of you..."

"Go, Niall, go. Bring extra salt if you can find any. I have mustard, and plenty of tea."

Everything faded to grey. This was death then. Farewell

Mette.

* * *

Time passed in darkness, interspersed by brief moments of awareness when someone sat him up and poured strong, salty tea in him. He gagged at the saltiness. "Try to keep it down, Frank," he heard Mette say once. She'd tilted his head back and forced something down his throat, but liquid still dribbled from the corners of his mouth. Then they rolled him over when his bladder was bursting and helped him urinate. "The colour's getting better."

He awoke suddenly into daylight. He'd been dragged into the tent and covered with Mette's once precious but now ruined quilt. The pain and cramping had gone, but he was exhausted, barely able to keep his eyes open.

"Mette?"

Joey had been lying beside him, unnoticed. He sat up and yelled, "Mumma, muma!"

The tent flaps were thrown open. "You're awake."

"Thirsty," he murmured.

She crawled in, smiling, kissed him on the forehead and cradled his head in her arms. "*Kaereste*! We thought you'd never wake up. I've never seen you sleep like that. Is your stomach better?"

He nodded and put his hand on hers where it lay on his chest. "What's…going on?"

"Niall's been helping me. I don't know what I would have done without him. He knew what to give you, and he stayed awake all night with me, forcing warm salted tea into you. He told me his father had a mixture of boiled tea and salt that he'd prepared for the cows in case they wandered near the fences. But they'd never had to use it and he wasn't sure it would work."

He cleared his throat. His mouth felt like the floor of a stable. "I've been out of it for one night? It feels more like a week. Can you give me some water?"

"There's a cup of beside you. We've been giving you that since your urine turned back to a normal colour. Since the sun came up. Joey, go and fill it for Frank."

Joey grabbed the cup and crawled from the tent. He returned with a full cup and helped Frank drink from it.

"That will help clear you out," said Mette. "Niall said we'd be able to tell you were getting better by watching the colour of your urine."

"God. How did you see my urine?"

"We rolled you over and you went in the billy that had the milk in it. We didn't want to use the billy anyway. We threw the milk in the creek, like Niall suggested."

He groaned. "Sorry. Mustn't have been easy for you, pushing me around like that."

"You are a bit heavy. But Niall helped. And Joey, of course, didn't you Joey? He was very worried about you."

"What did you do with our…other suspects? Who's with them?"

"Hemi's been guarding them with your revolver. Just Mr. and Mrs. Burns and Arthur of course. We're not treating Niall like a suspect any more."

He nodded and closed his eyes. "My head still hurts like hell. Could I sleep some more?"

"Would you like me to bring you a cup of tea?"

"I don't think I'll drink tea again for the rest of my life."

He gulped down the rest of the water and fell back to sleep.

He awoke to the sound of angry words.

"How much longer do we have to put up with this?"

He dragged himself through the tent opening. "Something the matter, Burns?"

"Ah, Sergeant Hardy. We've been sitting here all night and half the morning. I was wondering when you'd be back to take charge. Hemi has kept that damn revolver pointed at me the entire time. And we've had absolutely nothing to eat."

"I was afraid there'd be more poison," said Mette.

"It'd be hard to put poison on some things," said Arthur. "You could throw some potatoes in the fire and we could just eat the inside, not the skin."

"How would you know that, Arthur?" asked Burns.

He shrugged. "Stands to reason."

Burns glared at him. "Perhaps it was you who put the poisoned oats in the milk. It certainly wasn't me. And the Hardy's have apparently decided it wasn't Niall who killed his father, although why they would think that I don't know. If anyone had a reason…"

"Mette, do you have some potatoes you could throw in the fire?"

She disappeared into the supply tent and came out with her apron loaded with potatoes, which she pricked with a fork and tossed into the embers.

"They'll be ready in an hour." she said. "And we should have something to drink. Hemi, give Frank the revolver and get some water from the butt. Check it to make sure nothing is floating in it."

As Hemi handed him the revolver, Frank said quietly, "Hemi, don't mention the lost gun to anyone."

"I didn't," he whispered. "I think Niall has it. I know he's worried about someone trying to kill him."

Frank checked to make sure his gun was still loaded, and sat with it held it across his knee, dangling loosely from two fingers. His strength was returning, although his gut muscles ached.

"Now, this is what I know," he said to Burns. "You had a damn good reason to kill James O'Halloran. You could have slipped by me and up to the pasture when I wasn't looking. And your wife isn't the best witness for you because she spends most of her time asleep."

Burns rubbed his eyes and sighed. "Of course I disliked O'Halloran. I've never tried to hide the fact. But I'm not a killer, and I would hope you could tell that. And, more to the point, why would I poison everyone? For what reason? It makes no sense."

Frank nodded. "I can't see why you'd want to. The only possibility that occurs to me is that your wife did it in an attempt to kill you, and…"

He stopped as Burns looked sharply at his wife and said, "Grace…?"

Frank pressed home his advantage. "You thought your husband killed O'Halloran, didn't you?" he asked. "You were the only one who turned down the milk."

"Milk upsets my stomach. I said that at the time." She laid her hand on her husband's arm. "Jeremiah, surely you don't think I would do something like that."

"You've been hell bent on killing yourself," he said, pulling himself away from her

131

"Just the one time," she said softly. "And I was very, very upset."

"Of course you were," said Mette. "Why wouldn't you be, after killing your daughter accidentally."

They both turned on her.

"Who told you that?"

"Arthur mentioned it," said Frank. "He said you were tried for infanticide and the judge would have let you off if it weren't for O'Halloran persuading the jury that you should be punished in some way."

Mr. and Mrs. Burns looked at each other, puzzled.

"How would Arthur know?" asked Mrs. Burns.

"Pania told me," said Arthur.

"I'll have to talk to her about that…she should know better…" Grace Burns voice trailed off, and she sniffed and wiped her eye.

Her husband was not done with her. "Arthur knows you tried to kill yourself by throwing yourself off the carriage. So it was more than once."

"No I didn't. I had no intention of throwing myself…I lost my balance, didn't I Arthur? You tried to pull me back, I know, and I'm thankful. But somehow I found myself in the water. The carriage was tipping, surely."

"Ah, yes," said Arthur. "Of course. And I tried to pull you back." He raised his eyebrows at the others and grinned.

"Perhaps you tried to push her off," said Burns. "If my wife and I aren't responsible and if it wasn't Niall, that leaves you."

"Why isn't it Niall?" asked Arthur. "Let's face it, his father wasn't the best of men, and I'm sure Niall had good reason to kill him. He's a big, strong lad, and…"

"It wasn't Niall," Mette and Hemi said in unison.

"In that case," said Arthur stiffly, "it must have been one of the Burnses, because it certainly wasn't me. I have no reason to kill anybody. I've hardly been in the country. I don't know anyone here."

"It wasn't me, either," said Niall, who had been following the discussion from beside the fire, poking at the potatoes with a stick to keep them in the hottest part of the ashes. "I know I might have a reason to kill my father, but I didn't. And why would I want to kill everyone by poisoning the milk?"

"You got a taste for killing," said Arthur. "I've seen it happen. You kill once and then…"

"This is not helpful," said Frank. "And I can't see how I can get an answer. The only thing I can do is take the two of you - Mr. and Mrs. Burns - in to Feilding and let the police sort it out."

"Why not take Arthur as well?" asked Burns. "Would you leave him here with your wife? Do you trust both him and Niall?"

Frank sighed. His head was throbbing and he was ready for sleep again. He was sure he couldn't manage three prisoners all the way to Feilding. "Niall, have you been down to your barn in the last twenty-four hours? Has the water started to recede?"

"I was there getting salt last night," said Niall. The water's pulling back. What's left of the foundations of the house is covered in mud, but the rest of the place isn't bad. I think the route to Feilding is probably passable if you stay above the road for as long as you can. You could ride along the ridge for a mile or two."

"Good. I can't see any other choice but to take the Burnses into Feilding. Niall, I'll take my horse, Copenhagen and one of your horses with me. Mr. and Mrs. Burns, you can ride together. It'll take us a couple of hours to get to Feilding, and I'll come back as fast as I can." He laid his hand on Mette's shoulder. "Mette, will you be alright for a few hours? You aren't starting yet, are you?"

"I don't think so," she said. "I'll separate everyone and keep them busy until you return. Are you taking your rifle with you? Only, I don't like the thought of having a gun here."

"I'll take the ammo and leave my rifle in the storage tent. It won't be any use to anyone without ammo."

Jeremiah Burns stood outside his tent, his thumbs hooked in his waistcoat as if the action would stop Frank from dragging him away. "I'm not sure I agree with this plan, Sergeant Hardy. I'm quite sure I didn't murder anyone, and my wife certainly didn't murder Mr. O'Halloran. She wouldn't have the strength. He was a big, strong man who could easily overcome her. If she didn't commit the one murder, there's no reason for her to have committed the other."

"What would you suggest I do?"

"Take all the men in, and leave the women and children here. The police in Feilding can interview everyone and decide who they think is guilty, and the rest of us can ride back."

Frank glanced around the group. "In other words, you want me to leave my pregnant wife in charge of the boys and your insane, drug-addicted wife."

"How dare you."

"Keeping in mind that there are wild dogs roaming the countryside, and that there's still a remote chance that the killer is not one of this party...no, I'd like Niall and Hemi here, and Mrs. Burns with me. I'd take Arthur as well, but I'm not completely sure that you didn't hire him to kill O'Halloran..."

He did not want to say that he didn't think he could manage three of them. No need to give Burns any ideas about making a break for it.

"A hired killer? Me?" said Arthur. "Nice work if you can get it, I'm sure. How much does it pay? Any idea?"

Everyone glared at Arthur, and Mr. Burns sighed.

"Well, if that's what you think is best. I know I'll feel safer away from here."

* * *

Mette watched Frank as he rode up to the ridge with the Burnses. He held the traces of their horse, and had tied the reins around the horses's neck in a slip knot, out of reach of both of his prisoners. If Mr. Burns decided to spur the horse away from Frank and try to escape, he would have no way to influence the direction it took. And if he decided to leap backwards off the horse like a cowboy and make a run for it, he would first have to negotiate his way around his wife. She was confident they would arrive safely in Feilding.

She turned to the three boys and Arthur. "Now, I want everyone to keep busy until Frank comes back. Arthur, could you go down to the house and start sweeping the mud out the front door? You'll find a broom in the stable. We're going to have to scrub the floors and walls with carbolic soap, but getting rid of the mud before it dries and hardens will be a good start."

He nodded and saluted her. "Of course, Mrs. Hardy. Happy to help."

She didn't imagine he'd get much done, but at least it would keep him a good distance from the campsite. And there was no more whisky to be had. She had given the last of it to Grace Burns. She imagined he would spend his time checking the cupboards in the kitchen.

"Joey, you can stay with me. We're going to start collecting things that can be taken back to the house. We'll fill the wheelbarrow and push it down. Niall and Hemi, you'd better go and milk the cows again. And take the horse and foal with you. They're running out of grazing here and there's lots in the pasture. Be careful with Dolores. Make sure she's near the water. She can hardly move, poor thing."

"Should we keep the milk?" asked Niall.

"Take two of the tin cups with you and drink some yourselves. Throw the rest away for now. There'll be more tomorrow. Do either of you have a weapon?"

Niall looked guilty. "I have Hemi's gun," he said. "He left it behind yesterday. I didn't want to tell you in front of Sergeant Hardy because he'd think I was stupid. But I keep thinking someone's watching me and wants to kill me. So I put it in a secret place only I know about. It's safe, but Sergeant Frank might think…"

"Don't worry," said Hemi. "I told him I thought you had it. He wasn't angry. But why did you empty out the ammo bag?"

Niall patted the pocket of his vest. "I have the pellets in here. I thought if I was the only person who could use the gun I'd know I was safe."

"Good thinking," said Mette. "Off you go then. Show Hemi where the gun is so you can both get to it. And give him half of the pellets. And take Frank's rifle with you as well. It's in the storage tent and I hate seeing it there. He took the ammo with him. Apparently you and Frank think alike, Niall."

She stood with her hand on Joey's shoulder and watched them leave for the cow pasture.

"Now, Joey, we have some work to do. Let's make a pile of things that can safely go back to the house."

"I'm going to take my books back," he said. "I've read both of them twice."

"That's a good start. We can take the two billies, as well. Once they're cleaned out with carbolic soap they'll be fine."

"Even the one Sergeant Frank used for…?"

"Even that," she said firmly. "No use wasting a good billy can."

"I won't ever drink milk again, I don't think," he said. "Mumma, do you think it was Mrs. Burns who tried to poison us? I thought Mr. Burns was right when he said he had no reason to do it. It must have been Mrs. Burns."

"Well, someone did," said Mette. "I suppose it could be her. I hope not."

"So do I," said Joey. "I want her to show me how to draw. I hope it's either Mr. Burns or Arthur."

Mette shook her head sadly. "Unfortunately, I think Frank is probably right. Mr. Burns killed Mr. O'Halloran, and then his wife tried to poison us. I can't think of any reason for that not to be the case. She's a very unhappy woman and he's angry, although he doesn't show it."

15

Riding to Feilding

Frank kept to the ridge that started above the campsite. The farmland he glimpsed through the bush still looked swampy, and he knew how hard it could be riding in mud. He would stay on the ridge for as long as possible and head downhill when saw the Feilding road. He was feeling increasingly tired and weak, and wondered if he was up to the ride into Feilding and back. What if he was wrong about Burns?

Leaving Mette, Joey and Hemi with Arthur and Niall had seemed like a reasonable idea, but as he got further away from the campsite he began to experience doubts. What if he was wrong? Burns had an obvious reason to kill O'Halloran, but Niall was also a strong suspect. And what about Arthur? What did they know about him? The poisoning could be accidental, or someone - Arthur possibly - be out to make mischief for no reason. He tried to sort out all the clues as he rode, but his brain felt woolly and unfocused.

The ridge above the campsite was narrow - barely wide enough for Copenhagen to find her footing. He had tied a leading rope to O'Halloran's horse, but was forced to trust the horse to follow him. The track - if you could call it that - was thick with towering cabbage trees and difficult to navigate.

When the track widened, he reined in his horse and fell back beside his prisoners, holding the other horse close so he could navigate around the trees.

Mr. Burns held his wife in front of him, his eyes fixed on the road ahead, his expression one of resignation and sorrow. "Do you intend to take us to the Feilding gaol, Sergeant Hardy? That will be very hard on my wife."

Frank nodded, not looking at Burns, but concentrating on the track. He hoped Burns did not understand how weak he was. He could barely keep himself upright on his horse. Fortunately, Copenhagen understood him well, and trod carefully along the rutted hilltop.

"Well, I hope when we reach Feilding you'll inform my solicitor that I'm at the gaol. Samuel Goodbehere. He has an office on Manchester Square, where the Bank of Australasia used to be. Tell him I need his help…again."

"Why do you have a solicitor in Feilding?" asked Frank. "Wouldn't it make more sense to have one in Foxton? And come to that, why were you driving to Feilding to buy laudanum three days ago? Why not Foxton?"

"He was recommended to me by Arthur Halcombe, the immigration agent. Your wife would know him. He brought the Danes to Manawatu. He used to lease Sir William's farm at Westoe. I'd seen Goodbehere at the Horticultural Shows - he's the president of the Feilding society - and thought he looked like a decent fellow. And when I needed a solicitor - he came down to Foxton to represent Grace at the trial."

Frank was finding it hard to take it all in. Now that Burns was talking, he was saying too much. "And your reason for going to the dispensary in Feilding?"

Grace Burns twisted round in the saddle so she could see her husband. "You should tell the sergeant the whole story. I can't help but think the best way to prove our innocence is to be completely honest."

"You should listen to your wife, Burns."

"You know almost everything," said Burns. "But I suppose you're right. After the trial and my wife's first suicide attempt, the people of Foxton turned against us. Even the friend my wife was staying with when our daughter died. I believe the men on the jury paid attention to O'Halloran, and after the trial they talked to their wives, and the story got out. By the time Grace was transported to Wellington to be committed, no one in town was speaking to us in the street. I was cut so many times - it was shocking to me that people I'd known for years pretended they didn't know me. All the fault of O'Halloran, of course."

"That was part of the reason I tried to drown myself," said Grace Burns. "I couldn't bear to see Jeremiah treated that way, especially after we had suffered so much by losing Jane. I thought without me he would fare better."

"Thank you, my dear. I didn't know that was why…"

"The dispensary…?" prodded Frank, although he already knew the answer.

"The dispensary in Foxton refused to supply Grace with laudanum. I suppose it's obvious. The chemist knew about Jane and thought Grace might try something similar with someone…with me perhaps."

"I wouldn't, Jeremiah," said Grace. "You've been so good to me. As if I would do anything to hurt you." She turned to Frank. "I wasn't trying to poison Jeremiah, and why would I if it meant I would risk killing Mette and Joey as well? Joey is a dear little boy, and your wife has been so kind to me. I believe she's shown me a way to cure myself of my addiction."

The ridge broadened into a flattened hilltop. They could see Feilding in the distance now, a faint smudge of houses and buildings on the horizon. The Feilding road appeared to their left, mud-covered but passable. In one area, several swollen sheep carcasses had been loaded into a pile and set alight. The cleanup had begun, and the smell of rotting flesh mixed with burning kerosene was sickening. Knowing it would be worse on the road, he guided the horses downhill.

"You could let me take the reins, sergeant," suggested Burns, who was having a problem keeping his seat on the saddle. "I can't see how I could outrun you even if I wanted to. You're a more experienced rider with a much stronger horse, and Grace would slow me down."

Frank leaned over and untied the knot. His hand was trembling, and he was relieved Burns did not seem to notice his increasing weakness. "Keep talking," he said. "Grace was taken to Wellington, to the asylum. And then what?"

"Yes. It was a horrendous place. Dirty, crowded. I paid for extra food, but discovered that most of it was stolen before it reached her. I was desperate to get her out. I had to debase myself before Sir William."

So far Burns had made a good case for his own guilt. Of course, if Mette found herself in a similar situation he'd kill O'Halloran, and probably the same way. He remembered the knife thrust through the tongue, the message obvious: keep your mouth shut.

"And Sir William wrote to the governor of the asylum and

asked for Grace to be set free?"

"He did, although somewhat reluctantly. He had no idea of the conditions there until I informed him. As a temperance man, he disapproved of addiction of any kind. I believe he brought it up in the House afterwards - the conditions at the asylum - and improvements have been made. But laudanum is ninety percent alcohol, and he was more concerned about that than he was about the opium."

They rode in silence for several minutes, then Burns said, "Make sure your wife doesn't become addicted to any of the patent medicines, Hardy. She spoke about her sister using a cream on her children - Holloway's I believe. And she has her own mixture..."

"Her mixture is safe," said Frank with more confidence than he felt. "She makes it herself from ground willow bark and honey. I can't imagine it would be harmful. And it was recommended to her by a friend of her family who is a highly-respected physician in Haderslev." Secretly, he had doubts about her concoctions, but considering his own love of beer and whisky felt he was in no position to blame her for wanting something that dulled pain. In fact, he wished he had some of her mixture right now, to ease the pain of his aching stomach muscles. Better still, he wished he had a shot of the whisky that Arthur and Grace Burns had polished off between them.

"Queen Victoria chews gum laced with cocaine," said Grace. She was regaining her strength at the same rate Frank was losing his. "Or so I heard. My friend in Foxton has a friend in London who spends time at the palace. She says some of the ladies-in-waiting smoke opium in pipes, but the queen thinks that looks too manly."

"The friend she speaks of is the one who got her started on

laudanum, soon after she gave birth," said Burns. "I wouldn't necessarily believe her." Frank saw Grace flinch, as if he'd struck her.

"Giving birth was extremely painful," she said. "You have no idea how painful…Queen Victoria uses chloroform when she…"

"You took laudanum during childbirth?" asked Frank. Had she needed to do that? Was it that painful? What about Mette, then? He'd been concerned about her survival, but she was strong and healthy and he knew she'd make it through. But pain had not entered his mind. He'd spent most of his life in the company of men, and had seen how they dealt with pain. Was he going to have to watch her go through the kind of pain he'd seen wounded men suffer with no idea how to help her?

"No," said Grace. "But afterwards I was very sad, and my friend told me it would improve my mood. I took it for a while, but I was sleepy all the time and stopped. And then… and then…"

And then she'd rubbed the laudanum on her baby's gums, to stop the pain of teething, Frank thought. Not the only woman to do that, and probably not the first child who had died from a laudanum overdose. He read newspaper stories about it regularly. He was surprised she hadn't heard the stories herself. Of course, most women didn't read newspapers, other than the ladies' pages. Mette was the exception, as she was in so many ways.

A mile outside Feilding they came upon a gang of men repairing a cluster of downed telegraph lines. Unable to pass, they watched as a crew of three raised each pole with three guide ropes, after which an electrician on a raised platform on a cart pulled the line up onto the pole and hitched it around the insulator. A hundred yards away, on a small rise, a rifleman with his weapon across his knees sat watching them. A uniformed volunteer, but not anyone Frank knew.

"Why the guard?" he asked one of the workers.

"Animals, mostly," he said. "They're starving and the smell of our bread and sausages is driving them crazy."

"We were attacked by a wild dog," said Frank. "I suppose you've seen a few of those."

The worker nodded towards the ditch. "There's a big one in there. The marksman got it earlier today. One shot from that distance. Amazing young fellow. A champion shot. And there was a bull on the road nearer to town that went for us. Hated to see it go, but it wouldn't stop charging us. The owner's going to be demanding compensation from the council."

"Don't forget about the humans," the electrician called from above.

The worker laughed awkwardly. "We've seen a few hungry waifs go by, but we'd hardly shoot them, would we Fred?" He sounded unsure.

"That's really why that bloke is over there," said the electrician, gesturing at the rifleman with his head. "Not just for the animals. They had to empty out the gaol, and there's a couple of villains roaming the countryside."

"That could be your answer, sergeant," Burns said. "An escaped prisoner."

Frank shook his head. "Doesn't work," he said. "A prisoner would be more concerned with putting distance between himself and his gaoler. What use would it be to murder O'Halloran and attempt to poison the rest of us?"

"Murder? Poison?" asked the worker. "What's going on?"

"Nothing I can talk about," said Frank. "I need to get into town and find the local constable. Who is it, do you know? I heard there'd been transfers and someone new was coming to Feilding."

"Constable Price, from Palmerston. He was sent here last month. He has his hands full today, I'll bet."

"Excellent," said Frank. "I've known Price for years."

The crew cleared the road and moved to the next felled pole.

"Two more poles," said the electrician. "And then telegrams from Palmerston will be coming along the lines. Everyone in the district will be shouting for help. Just what we need. You can go ahead, sir. Watch out for bulls and wild dogs."

Frank navigated around them, followed by Mr. and Mrs. Burns, and headed into town.

Feilding buzzed with activity. The streets were still muddy, and there were signs that water had been up over verandahs, but women were scrubbing steps and men were hurrying from the timber yard with loads of planks on their drays. The race course, where Frank spent so much time in the season, looked more like a lake than a racetrack. He wondered if it would be cleaned in time for the opening. So much work. He was dreading the thought of it.

They slogged through the mud to the police station and dismounted. As he slid off Copenhagen his knees gave way, and he grabbed her saddle to keep himself upright. Burns was talking to his wife, both of them looking very serious, and didn't notice. Once he regained control over his legs, he strode over to the station and pounded on the door. A sleepy-looking sub-constable, not much older than Niall, answered the door. He was alone, having been left in charge for the day. He came out and stared at Mr. and Mrs. Burns curiously.

"I need you to keep a couple locked up until I can speak with Constable Price. Do you know where he is?"

The sub-constable wiped his nose with the back of his hand. "These two? Locked up? Are they crooks? They don't look like crooks."

"Constable Price?" Frank reminded him.

"He's at the Feilding Hotel with the work parties," said the sub-constable. "They're having a quick break for sandwiches. It's on the corner of Denbigh Square and the Kimbolton Road. Do you..."

"I know it. Thanks."

He dragged himself back on his horse and said to the sub-constable, "I won't leave them here. I'll take them to the hotel with me. Maybe Constable Price can arrange more agreeable lodgings there. I really don't want to see Mrs. Burns in the lockup."

Constable Price was standing in the dining room with a group of sturdy Scandinavian axemen from the Manchester Block who had been assembled to remove fallen trees from the Kimbolton Road. A table loaded with sandwiches and mugs of beer had been moved to the centre of the room. Several of the Scandies were already attacking the food. Price greeted Frank tiredly and listened to his story.

"Have a sandwich," he said to the Burnses, "and then I'll put you in a room down the hall. You'll be comfortable there for a day or so."

Mr. and Mrs. Burns sat down and nodded to the men already seated. One offered Mr. Burns a glass of beer, but he shook his head firmly and asked for a cup of tea. From the way he was acting, he was not especially upset about his situation, but it was hard to tell. The evidence was going to be all circumstantial, and he would know he was likely to go free. A good lawyer would have no problem keeping the pair of them out of prison.

Constable Price sat next to Frank, out of earshot of the Burnses. "I'll keep them here," he said. "We've got a couple of recaptured prisoners from the lockup in rooms down the hallway with a guard outside. We picked them up this morning. A pathetic pair. I arrested them for forgery a couple of days ago. Tried to buy some gin with a bank note drawn in pencil which fooled absolutely no one. They were counting on the darkness of the bar to fool the owner."

Frank ate a plate of sandwiches and washed it down with a pint of beer. His strength and energy returning, he walked to Manchester Square and left a message for Samuel Goodbehere telling him his client Jeremiah Burns required his urgent attendance at the Feilding Hotel.

Returning to the hotel to retrieve the newly fed and watered Copenhagen, he ran into the young sub-constable from the lockup. He was clutching a telegram and looked worried.

"Is Constable Price still at the hotel?" he asked.

"He was there ten minutes ago," said Frank. "Have you got more bad news for him?"

"Another escaped prisoner," said the sub-constable.

"What did this one do? Indulge in some furious riding?"

"It's not local," said the sub-constable. "It's someone who escaped from Pentridge Gaol in Melbourne. Took advantage of the Kelly hanging when there were so many people around wanting to see the body. Killed a guard, then lied himself aboard the Ruahine. Claimed he was an experienced cook, and they needed one, because their cook had gone missing. They found him floating in the harbour after the boat had sailed. The escapee was last seen in Wellington, and they believe he was heading up the coast on the Stormbird. The Stormbird comes up the west coast, so he's probably up in Wanganui or New Plymouth, but he could have got off in Foxton, in which case…"

Frank felt a rush of nervous energy, tinged with terror, flood through his body. "Do you know his name? Or what he looks like?"

The sub-constable held open the telegram and read it carefully. "Tall, very thin. Name of O'Connor. Arthur O'Connor."

16

Joey's Book

The wheelbarrow was almost full. Mette and Joey had piled it with bedding from the Burnses' tent, and plates and cutlery from the supply tent. Everything would need a good wash before being used again, and she could get started today before she was forced to rest for two weeks. Her washboard and soap were in the washhouse behind the stable and she would ask lazy Arthur to carry it into the yard for her. He would at least do that.

Her beautiful quilt, which she had taken into her own tent to cover Frank when he lay there suffering, looked almost beyond repair. What with being draped around Mrs. Burns for several days, and on top of Frank as he vomited and passed water all night, she could see it would never again be good enough to be stored in the chest for special occasions. She would take it down to the house and wash it gently with the bar of Castile soap Frank had bought her for her birthday, but it would never be special again.

Although, on second thoughts, perhaps it had been used for a special occasion. What could be more special than keeping Frank warm while he recovered from a dose of arsenic poisoning? The thought cheered her up.

She threw the quilt on top of the other blankets in the wheelbarrow. "Let's take this lot down to the house," she said to Joey. "I'll get Arthur to help us unload everything and put it away."

"Didn't Sergeant Frank say you shouldn't push the wheelbarrow?" he said. "I can do it by myself. I'm strong."

"He meant uphill," she said. "We'll be going downhill and all we'll have to do is keep it going straight. It will run by itself. Why don't you take one handle and I'll take the other. It will be easier that way."

In spite of what she expected, it wasn't easy. Guiding a wheelbarrow downhill was actually more difficult than pushing it uphill; she had to bend forward awkwardly and walk quickly to keep up with it as it wobbled from side to side. She was panting when they reached the house, with a stitch in her side and aching calves.

"I need to rest for a minute, Joey," she said. "I can't walk any more."

"Would you like to lean on me?"

She looked around. The pitchfork was still leaning against the stable, where she'd left it after she stabbed the eel. "Bring me the pitchfork. I can lean on the handle."

They hobbled into the house together, Joey trying hard to help, but actually getting in the way.

"Arthur? Are you here?"

She heard a loud snort from her bedroom, as if someone was sleeping there.

"Frank? Is that you?"

She grimaced at Joey and whispered, "It must be Arthur. I

think he's asleep. What a lazy person he is."

She opened the door to the bedroom. Arthur was lying on the bed, his mouth open, snoring loudly. He had moved her precious spring mattress from where it had been leaning against the wall and put it back on the bed. The bed she shared with Frank.

"Arthur!"

His eyes shot opened. "Oh, hello there Mrs. Hardy. I got tired, what with all the work and that bang on the head. I thought I'd take a little nap. This mattress is very comfortable, I must say. I hope you don't mind me using it. I took my shoes off so I wouldn't get it muddy."

She did mind, very much. The fact that he had taken off his shoes to avoid getting the mattress muddy only made things worse. He wore no socks and his feet were filthy. What really annoyed her was that he had made himself at home, and showed no remorse now she had caught him.

She did her best to hide her irritation, but could not keep a certain briskness out of her voice. "Would you please get up and help me bring in some of the things Joey and I wheeled down from the camp?"

He stood up reluctantly and stretched. "Well, back to work, I suppose."

The floor was still covered with a thick layer of mud. He had obviously not done the tiniest bit of work. There was no sign of the broom he was supposed to have fetched from the stable.

"Joey," she said pointedly. "Hop out to the stable and bring me the broom. Arthur can start pushing out some of this mud."

"Alright then, mumma," said Joey. "I'll be right back."

As he spun around and ran out the bedroom door, something dropped from his pocket and fell into the mud. His book.

Mette lowered herself awkwardly, balancing on the pitch-fork, and picked it up. "Oh dear. It's all muddy."

She slapped it against her skirt, and then realized there was a clump of something caught in the pages. Leaves, she thought. She opened the book.

And saw Arthur's face looking at her from the page.

The story beside the pen-and-ink sketch was long and involved and it took her a while to take it all in. Queen Victoria. The Irish Guard. Brave John Brown. A young man with his hand on Victoria's coach who had followed the queen into the palace grounds pretending to be part of her entourage.

Hardly able to breathe, she looked up at Arthur. He was staring down at the open page of the book. He lifted his eyes slowly to meet hers; his lids were drooped, the look on his face bemused. His thinness suddenly seemed like a strength, as if a starving cat had turned into a panther.

"Well, then," he said. "Now you know. Unfortunately."

"You tried to assassinate Queen Victoria?"

He shrugged. "Not really. I was trying to hand her a note, and she took it."

"But you had a gun."

"Empty," he said. "I was just trying to make a point. She understood. Looked me right in the eye and said she would do what I asked. But that bloody man of hers, John Brown, he jumped from the carriage and tackled me, and I hit back at him. It was all a big misunderstanding - all I wanted was for her to read a petition to free the Fenians. I'm Irish, you know, and come from a famous Irish family. I wanted to restore the glory of the family name. The constabulary didn't understand, of course. They accused me of trying to murder her and sent me to Australia - the queen requested specifically that they not hang me. But I wanted them to hang me...to go down in history as a great patriot."

"And Mr. O'Halloran was there? He saw what happened?"

"He was with the Irish Guards. They threw me onto a gun carriage and took me off to their guardhouse. He was riding beside the carriage, so he had a good look at me. And then in the yard in the dark the other night he recognized me. What else could I do? I can't go back to Australia. My life there was hell. It was him or me."

She kept her eyes on his but mentally checked the rest of the room to see what she could use to distract him. In the meantime, the best she could think of was to keep him talking. She leaned on the pitchfork and said, "Mr. Burns will be disappointed that he hired you, after all that he and his wife have been through. It's a pity we can't let them know..."

He chuckled. "Nothing for you to worry about. You won't have a chance to tell anyone. We'll just wait for young Joey to get back with the broom, and that will be it. I'll leave you both on the mattress you care about so much."

A rush of relief coursed through her body. He was going to tie them up and leave them on the bed. Then she saw something in his eyes that had always been there, but that she had never noticed before. A spark of something. Madness? Suppressed rage? She wasn't sure. But she knew in an instant he was not going to tie them up on the bed. He was going to kill them both.

He took something from his pocket. One of her carving knives, the small one that she had foolishly left in the drawer, even after the large one had been used to kill Mr. O'Halloran.

He rubbed it against his palm. "Quite sharp, isn't it? I suppose Sergeant Hardy has kept it well-honed. The large one worked a treat. I hardly put any effort at all in shoving it into the lying throat of that bastard O'Halloran. He asked me to meet him up in the pasture early in the morning. Suggested we could discuss my 'problem'. He was going to take me on as a hired man and work me to death forever."

She dropped the book back into the mud, pretending it had slipped from her fingers. But she held the pitchfork tightly. An idea was forming in her mind.

He looked down at the book regretfully. "Who would have thought that I would find someone who recognized me and a book about me in the same…"

Taking advantage of his brief inattention, she raised the pitchfork and drove it hard into his bare left foot just above his toes. Before he could react, she angled it at her stomach and leaned on the handle using all her weight to push it further in. She felt something give and then stop. The pitchfork had hit the wooden floor beneath his foot.

He tried to take a step, but he was pinned to the floor with blood oozing from the wound.

"You bitch," he said. "I was going to off you gentle, but not any more. You and your Maori spawn. He'll go first and you can watch him squeal like a pig."

She wrenched the pitchfork out as roughly as she could and backed out the door. He took a step after her and fell back onto the bed, clutching at his wound. Without the tines of the pitchfork to plug the wound, blood gushed from his foot.

"Shit."

She backed out of the bedroom, slammed the door, shoved the tines into the floor as hard as she could, then wedged the handle under the door handle. She could hear him cursing. He sounded as if he was still in the middle of the bedroom. As she prayed he would not be able to force the door open, he threw himself against it. The pitchfork wedged further into the wooden planks and held fast. With the door blocked, there was only one way he could get out of the house. He'd have to break the tiny bedroom window and pull himself through over broken glass. She had a tiny advantage.

She ran out into the yard and found Joey holding the broom, frozen to the spot, his face a mask of fear and panic.

She grabbed his hand and knocked the broom to the ground. "We have to go. Arthur is the killer. He's trapped in the bedroom and he'll need to stop the bleeding before he follows us. We have a head start. We'll go into the lane and get as far away as we can. "

He held her hand tightly and ran with her to the gate, not asking why Arthur was bleeding or how he had been trapped in the bedroom. She took a minute to close the gate after them, hoping it might cause Arthur to head in the opposite direction, but knowing they had left footprints in the mud leading to the gate. The most she could hope for was that he would head to the campsite without thinking about the gate and the lane that ran past the house, because he would know the creek was impassable.

The lane was not much more than a rutted track between high trees. Normally when they went into town they would cross the creek and turn onto the track down to the main road to Feilding. That would be the safe way to go. But the creek would stop them. They would have to go in the other direction.

She turned left out of the gate and ran up the lane, Joey flying along beside her. The lane meandered for a mile, rising and falling with the terrain, before ending in a field, but there were several paths running away through the bush by which they could make their way to the Feilding road. She'd walked that way looking for honey and edible fern roots many times. Once they were over the first rise, they would be hidden from view from the gate. She would pick the path that hid them best, and creep down it to the Feilding road. If they were lucky, they would meet Frank returning from Feilding.

But as they came to the top of the first rise, the lane ended abruptly in a sharp drop. It had collapsed into a muddy, impassable morass. To the south where she hoped to find a rescue she could see nothing but impenetrable bush; they would never be able to get to the road that way. The paths she had taken on her walks were much further on. If they tried to crawl around the edge of the collapsed road to get to those paths they could fall into the mud, and unless they could move very quickly they would be exposed to Arthur's view.

"We have to go back to the creek, Joey," she said. "And somehow get across." In her heart she knew they would never make it over the creek, but she couldn't think of any other way. Perhaps they could walk upstream.

They crept back along the fence to the gate. The bedroom window had been broken and something thrown across the sill to help Arthur climb out without cutting himself. There was no sign of him, however. "Let's get past the gate," she whispered. "He's not there. He must have gone the other way."

They ran to the creek, where just a few days ago she and Joey had stabbed the eel. She could hardly believe that so much had happened since then. The creek was churning slightly less than it had last time, and had less debris. If she had been alone she would have tried to cross. But with Joey it would take time, and they stood as much chance of being trapped there as they had in the other direction. She took a tentative step into the water.

"We'll be swept away if we go in there," said Joey. "What are we going to do, mumma? Is he going to kill us?"

Behind them, the gate gave a long, achingly slow creak as it was pushed open from the other side.

She pulled Joey closer. "*Pokkers*! He's coming."

He was going to kill them both. Too late to attempt to cross the creek. But there was one desperate way for them to save themselves. "Joey, we're going to have to jump in the creek and let it take us away from here."

"I can't, mumma. I can't swim."

"Hello, Mrs. Hardy," said a voice. "I was wondering where you were."

She turned and saw him hobbling towards her. He had cut a slice of cotton from the mattress and wrapped it around his foot and was using Frank's cricket bat as a walking stick. The knife was stuck in his belt, ready to be used as soon as he had them cornered.

She picked up Joey and leapt into the creek.

17

Back to the Farm

Constable Price was sitting on a bench outside the Feilding Hotel pulling on a pair of muddy riding boots when Frank arrived at a run, the sub-constable two steps behind him.

Price finished pulling on his boots and then scanned the telegram.

"He's on my property," said Frank. He was breathing heavily, trying to suppress his panic. "Burns brought him there. He's alone with Mette and the boys. But he doesn't know we're on to him. He's already murdered someone, a dairy farmer. And he may have murdered the farmer's wife as well."

Constable Price snapped his fingers at his subordinate. "Get a posse together, fast as you can. And horses. I'll recruit the Scandies with their axes. We'll meet back here. I'm sorry, Frank, but it may take me as much as an hour to get everyone moving. Go on ahead and have someone waiting on the road near the O'Halloran farm to tell us where you are. Do you have someone you can trust?"

"Hemi," said Frank. "You know Hemi, don't you? From the Pa?"

The publican had come out the front door of the hotel.

"Anything I can do to help?" he asked.

"If Mr. Goodbehere, the solicitor, turns up, tell him his clients can go free. But have them wait in Feilding for a day or two. We'll need to find out everything we can about Arthur O'Connor and they may have some insight. Constable Price will give you all the details while he's raising the posse."

"You're looking a little pale, Sergeant Hardy," said the publican. "Have you been ill?"

"Arsenic poisoning," said Frank. He dragged himself astride Copenhagen. His pain was irrelevant now. "But I'm well enough to get this criminal. I'll have my hands around his neck before the posse gets there."

"Try not to kill him," said Price, waving the telegram at Frank. "The Australian police are very keen to have him back alive so they can hang him. They want him for several murders, apparently."

The publican pulled a flask from his waistcoat pocket. "Take this. It will give you a boost when you need it. My best brandy."

Frank accepted it gratefully and took a swig. "Thanks. I need all the help I can get."

He spurred Copenhagen around and headed home, feeling as if he was caught in some kind of myth: he was Sisyphus, condemned to push a rock up a hill, only to have it roll back down. Just months ago, he'd made the ride from Patea to Palmerston in a panic, thinking Mette was alone on the farm with a killer. Now it was happening again. They had survived the last time; he kept telling himself they would survive once more.

He passed the dead bull - a shorthorn by the look of it - about a mile out of Feilding. The marksman had hit it in the chest with one shot, throwing it onto its back. If he'd had to stop the bull himself, he would have aimed for a shoulder, or something that would bring it to a halt without killing it. He might even have shot it in the ear, which could have had the desired effect. Good bulls cost twenty quid or more, and one bull could constitute someone's entire livelihood. The crew could probably have dodged it, or hidden behind their cart. Killing a bull was foolish.

A few miles further along the road, he came upon the telegraph crew in their cart, heading back to Feilding. The marksman rode beside them, and greeted him with a half salute. He was a young man, full of the confidence one saw from young men who didn't know any better.

"Didn't know it was you that went past before, Sergeant Hardy. I saw you ride in the volunteer parade a few months back."

"Are you finished for the day?"

"Looks like it," said the electrician. "The telegrams are passing through without a problem, so there aren't any more lines down."

"Could you come with me on a job?" Frank asked the marksman. "Constable Price is bringing a posse, but he's an hour behind me. There's a murder suspect on my farm, and my wife and boys are with him. I'm on the way to make sure he doesn't do anything before they get there."

The marksman swung his horse around. "Course I can." He was a big man, with a build not unlike Frank's. A good person to have on board, in spite of his youth, and, Frank suspected, lack of experience in the field.

"Let Constable Price know I have help," he told the telegraph crew. "We don't want them to shoot him accidentally."

"Good to be working with you, sergeant," said the marksman as they trotted together along the road away from Feilding. "My name is Brown. John Brown, can you believe it? I'm not about to be mouldering in the grave any time soon."

He laughed at his own joke. Obviously not the first time he'd used it. Frank and Mette had seen a performance by the Palmerston North Christy Minstrels at the Foresters Hall last year, and they'd enjoyed the beautiful rendition of that song, among others.

John Brown was clearly too young to have first hand knowledge of the American Civil War, and was certainly not old enough to have fought in the New Zealand Land Wars more than a decade ago. But at least he was a crack shot. "Where did you learn to shoot?" Frank asked.

"My father taught me," said Brown. "He was a soldier. He was wounded at the battle of The Beak of the Bird, back in '68. Taught me everything he learned during the war. Now I make a couple of pounds a week at matches and a bit more as a marksman - wild dogs and such. Keeps the farm going. Today was the first time I've had to guard against escaped prisoners, though. I'm glad I didn't have to shoot one of them."

Frank nodded. He doubted that this man's father had taught his son everything he knew. Shooting at men was not the same as shooting at a target or even at a wild dog or bull.

"Find yourself a high spot," he said. "But first, survey the entire area carefully. He doesn't know I know about him and he could be at the campsite in the paddock between the O'Halloran farm and my place…he's inclined to wander around though. My wife is there, so approach with caution."

John Brown's expression indicated that he thought he was

being lectured to on his area of expertise. But he nodded as if he'd taken everything in.

Frank couldn't help adding, with the bull in mind, "And remember you don't have to kill him unless he's actually threatening you. Shoot him in the leg. Bring him down. Don't go for the chest or the head."

"I don't know how I'd feel, killing a man," said Brown. "It must seem strange. Have you killed anyone, Sergeant Hardy?"

"In battle," said Frank. "And a couple of other times." It wasn't something he was proud of. And it also wasn't something he was ready to do again. However, if Arthur had harmed Mette, he'd pay for it with his life.

He gave Brown the rest of the details as they rode. He'd decided to return the same way he'd come, along the ridge, but sent Brown on the road to the O'Halloran farm. It would be harder going, but if he flushed Arthur down towards the road, Brown would be there to prevent him from getting away. He hoped young Brown wouldn't do to Arthur what he had done to the bull. He probably wouldn't have to. A weakling like Arthur with his thin, frail body wouldn't give him any trouble.

He came down from the ridge to the campsite with his gun drawn. He'd hoped to find Mette there working busily and unaware of the peril she was in. But the campsite was empty. He dismounted and checked the tents. Everything looked normal. No sign of any disturbance. The fire had almost burned out, and Mette had left mutton stew cooking in a Dutch oven. The stew was almost dry, and he used a handkerchief to pick it up the pot and move it to the ground. She'd thought she would be back soon, obviously. His cricket bat lay beside the fire, for what reason he couldn't fathom. It had been in his bedroom on the chest the last time he'd seen it. He went into each of the tents to make sure no one was there, silenced somehow. All were empty.

Back outside, he found a line in the mud heading up to the ridge, with footsteps either side. Mette and someone - Joey by the size of the footprints - had taken a loaded wheelbarrow down to the house. More footprints led to the pasture. Niall and Hemi had probably gone to milk the herd. No sign of Arthur, although he thought he could see a set of footprints mingled with the track of the wheelbarrow.

He remounted Copenhagen and trotted down past the paddock to his own yard. The wheelbarrow, loaded with blankets, sat next to the pump, covered by Mette's precious quilt. Footprints surrounded the wheelbarrow in every direction, and it was hard to read what had happened. He doubted she would leave the wheelbarrow sitting there and go and do something else. She must still be here.

Praying she was still alive, he drew his gun and opened the front door slowly. The parlour and the kitchen were empty, but the door to his and Mette's bedroom was jammed shut with a pitchfork. He stood close to the door and said quietly, "Mette?"

When no reply came, he braced himself with his gun in one hand, and pulled away the pitchfork with the other. The door came open, and he felt a breeze coming through the window. He stepped into the room and dropped the pitchfork.

Blood.

There was blood on the mattress and a pool on the floor beside the bed.

A large hole had been carved into the mattress cover and a piece removed. He was breathing heavily, trying to tamp down

163

his fear. What had happened? Had Arthur trapped Mette in the room? Was she bleeding…had she…no, not that, surely. It was too soon. Not for a couple of weeks.

The window looking out to the yard had been broken and a piece of the mattress cover draped across the broken glass on the windowsill. Someone had climbed out the window using the mattress cover to avoid being cut. Not Mette. She wouldn't fit through in her condition. Had Mette helped Joey out the window? If she had, where was she?

He closed his eyes and focused. The only thing that made sense was that Mette had trapped Arthur in the room with the pitchfork against the door, and that he had escaped through the window. Could the blood have come from the broken glass? No. There was too much blood, and it was on the mattress. She had wounded him somehow. What could she have used for a weapon?

The pitchfork.

He inspected the pitchfork, and found traces of blood on the tines. So she had stabbed him with it, and wounded him enough to cause heavy bleeding, but not enough to stop him from climbing out the window. She must have got him in the leg.

His spirits raised, he went back into the yard. From this angle, with the sun shafting in from the south, he could see footprints leading in the direction of the gate. Three sets of footprints, one set small, one set belonging to a woman by the look of the boot size, and a set of barefoot prints with something beside them that looked as if a cricket bat had been pressed into the ground. He remembered the bat he'd seen up at the campsite. Arthur had used it to break the window and then as a makeshift walking stick. That confirmed his suspicion that she had hurt his leg.

He flung open the gate and went out into the lane, hitching Copenhagen loosely to the gatepost.

The story in the lane was easier to read. Mette and Joey had run up the lane to the left, but for some reason had returned and gone to the creek.

Arthur's tracks went directly down to the water, with one footprint sinking deeper than the other. He was hobbling. She had wounded him in the foot, not the leg. The tracks went down beside the creek a short way, then stopped. Arthur had returned through the gate and into the yard - at a run, by the look of it. He bent and inspected Arthur's tracks more closely; he could see there was blood pooling in the indentations of his toes.

Beside the creek, he could see a heavier indentation. Joey's footprints disappeared and right next to his last step was one deep footprint beside the water. Mette had jumped into the creek holding Joey. He looked at the rampaging water and his spirits dropped again. How could they possibly survive in that?

He had to get to the O'Halloran farm as fast as he could without alerting Arthur, who could be hiding somewhere. Arthur would have rushed down to catch Mette as she came down. The tracks he had seen intermingled with the wheelbarrow tracks must have been heading up, not back.

The fastest way to get there, now that the water had receded, was to cross the creek and ride down by the track to the Feilding road. He'd avoid Arthur that way as well, and not alert him to the fact he'd returned. And if John Brown was already in place, sitting somewhere high, his rifle trained on the yard, he would be able to stop Arthur in his tracks. He wondered briefly why he hadn't heard a shot already. What was going on down there?

He ran back to the gate and untied Copenhagen. He stroked her mane encouragingly. "Come on old girl," he said. "You're going to show your skill as a steeplechaser."

He rode up the lane a short distance, turned, and eyed the creek. About ten feet across. He was almost sure Copenhagen could jump that far. She'd carried him through battles, leaping over ditches and enemy lines, often under a barrage of cannon fire. But she was older now, and hadn't jumped for years. He hoped her body remembered how to do it. He also hoped his body remembered how to do it.

He said a quick prayer, dug his heels into her side, and went for it.

Copenhagen flew across the creek and landed comfortably on the opposite side at a full gallop. He kept up the speed as they rounded the corner to the track south. The track was rutted but dry, and curved away to the Feilding road, connecting with it about a mile from the O'Halloran farm.

In spite of the muddiness of the Feilding road, he arrived at the farm faster than he had expected. He slowed Copenhagen to a trot, and rode up the long lane to the house, giving her a chance to recover. He hoped Brown had found himself a high spot from which to survey the property.

In the O'Halloran yard, Brown's riderless horse stood near the barn, untethered. He circled the yard on Copenhagen, his gun out, moving from side to side to make sure he didn't miss a movement. Where would Brown have gone? Had he chased after Arthur on foot?

Once he was sure neither Brown nor Arthur were in the yard

he dismounted and tied Copenhagen loosely to the rail in front of the barn. Then, keeping his back to the centre of the yard, he made his way around the perimeter again. Arthur O'Connor was out there watching him, he could feel his presence.

As he reached the patch of flattened hydrangeas that had been at the back of the house, he saw a faint outline of a person through the trees at the side of the creek. Someone in dun-coloured clothing wearing a broad-brimmed hat was sitting near the edge of the creek, turned away from the yard. He recognized Arthur's hat.

He watched for several minutes, not breathing, afraid he had already alerted him. Was it worth taking a shot at him while he wasn't looking?

But on second thoughts, what if it was Mette sitting there, recovering from a terrifying trip down from the place where she had gone into the water, or waiting for Joey? Even mourning Joey because he'd drowned? He wanted to call out, but stopped himself. He moved closer.

The person did not move.

Keeping his gun trained towards the creek, he crossed the yard. Whoever it was was sitting on a rock at the edge of the water, his or her feet in the creek. Was Arthur washing off the blood from his injured foot? He moved still closer, choosing his steps carefully so he made no sound.

And still the figure didn't move. Something was terribly wrong.

"Mette?"

The figure slumped forward into the water suddenly, thrown over by the current, and floated face down, arms by its side. The water tugged at the hat and it swirled away, revealing long, light-coloured hair. A woman. A woman wearing a brown dress. Not Sarah. She'd worn a white dress. Who then? It had to be Mette.

Without stopping to think about it, he shoved his gun into his belt and waded out into the creek.

18

Mette Washes Downstream

They were dragged along under the water, unable to breathe, or to have any influence on where the water took them. Mette's lungs were desperate for air. She had almost given in to the idea they were both going to die when suddenly they surfaced in a shallow pool above the last drop before the campsite. She sat in water up to her waist, coughing and gasping for air, unable to fill her lungs. Joey still clung to her.

"Are you alright, Joey?"

When he didn't reply, she threw him across her knee and pounded him on the back. He spluttered and started to drag in air desperately. "I couldn't breathe. I thought I was going to die."

She looked back upstream, and was shocked to see they had come no more than fifty yards. She could see Arthur through the overhanging bushes. He was working his way along the edge of the creek, choosing his steps carefully, holding on to branches with one hand, and supporting himself with Frank's cricket bat with the other. He had not seen them yet, or at least was making no attempt to conceal himself. He was looking at the ground, probably worried about where he was stepping.

"We've got to keep going, Joey."

"Can't we just get out here and run alongside the stream?"

She looked down the track beside the creek - what there was of it above the water. "If we do we'll be blocked by bushes and get trapped. I think we can move faster in the creek."

She waded to the edge of the pool, grabbed hold of a branch, and leaned out to see what was below, feeling the tug of the water as it spilled over the edge. A short drop, almost a waterfall, another deep pool, and then the cataclysm that tumbled the rest of the way down the hill to the O'Halloran farm. They could make it over the first drop, but the next part looked terrifying. But she could hear Arthur coming. Once again, they had no choice.

They slid over the edge of the pool and dropped into the water below, resting up to their waists. She pulled Joey towards her. "I'll hold you as tight as I can, and we're going to let ourselves go again. We made it this far. We'll be alright. I promise."

He nodded, shivering.

Holding him in a tight grip she threw herself out into the middle of the creek. The current caught them and they barrelled down the creek feet first. She had no time to think. All she knew was if she let go of Joey he would certainly drown. They were under water for several seconds, scraping against the stony bottom of the creek, then they were thrown above the surface briefly.

"Breathe, Joey," she yelled. She heard him suck in a breath, and then they were under water and spinning again.

It was over before she had time to worry. She saw a flash of willow branches above her head, then they came to an abrupt, jarring stop. Her legs were partially wedged under the roots of a willow, but the bulk of her belly, with Joey on top, had stopped her from being forced completely beneath the roots. Her feet had rammed into something soft; she felt whatever it was start to move. She moved with it, slipping beneath the roots. She had to stop herself; Joey would never be able to pull her out if she went under completely.

She rolled Joey away and pushed him out of the current. "Get up on the tree, quick, before we get sucked beneath the roots."

He scrambled up like a frightened rat and sat astride a branch, hugging himself. She could hear his teeth chattering above the sound of the water. He stared down at the creek as if he expected it to come up and pull him back in.

Without Joey on top of her she was able to move against the tug of the current. She wiggled backwards, a few inches at a time, until she was free from the tree. Now that she was no longer hurtling downstream, she had time to worry. Had her baby survived? She felt a tiny bit of movement, which was good, but her belly was tight, almost as if a snake had wrapped itself around her and was trying to strangle her.

The pull of the water was weaker away from the roots, but it still swirled around her insistently, trying to nudge her back into danger. Whatever she'd hit was no longer there. She pulled herself onto dry land and helped Joey move along the branch to the bank of the creek. Her body felt as if it weighed a ton and it took all her strength to move herself.

They sat huddled together without speaking. Then Joey said, his voice shaking, "Did we get away from the bad man, mumma?"

She nodded. "I think so. What did we hit? I felt something soft."

Joey sniffed and rubbed his eyes. "We hit the lady. She was under the tree."

Mette dragged herself to her feet and leaned out over the water wondering what Joey had seen. "The lady? I can't see anything."

"She went down the creek," he said. "I saw her when I was sitting on the branch." He moved closer to Mette and held her hand. "I'm glad it wasn't you."

Sarah, she thought. Frank had said she was lodged under a willow tree at the edge of the creek. She'd saved their lives. The realization hardened her determination. They were going to survive this. She would make sure they did. And she would find a way to make it up to Sarah.

"Let's go, Joey. When Arthur gets to the drop and doesn't see us he'll think we drowned or left the creek somehow. He'll head back towards the campsite. We need to find a place to hide where he won't look for us."

"Where can we go? Won't he find us anywhere we go?"

She thought desperately. Back to the house or the soddy, and barricade themselves inside? They needed more protection than that. Perhaps the boys could help? At least they had a gun of sorts. "We'll go to the pasture and find Hemi and Niall. Niall has Hemi's gun hidden somewhere, and he can protect us. Arthur's only weapon is a knife and there'll be four of us."

She didn't feel confident at all but dragged Joey through the trees towards the campsite pretending she was sure she was doing what was best for them. How quickly could Arthur get back to the house and up the path beside the paddock to the campsite? He would move fast, even limping and using his home made walking stick. He was unstoppable. He was probably already hobbling towards the camp, not far from where they were now.

She stopped at the edge of the bush near the campsite in heavy shade and squatted down amidst the ferns, pulling Joey down with her. "Let's wait here for a few minutes and see if he goes past."

"Shouldn't we just run for it?"

"I'd rather wait until I know where he is. Once he's passed us and gone down the hill to the O'Halloran's place he won't come back right away. He'll wait for us down there. We'll run for it then."

"He'll find the lady," said Joey.

An image flashed in Mette's mind of Arthur wading into the creek and pulling out Sarah's body, thinking it was her. She shuddered at the thought of his touch. Poor Sarah. Manhandled even in death. What would he do when he discovered it was Sarah? Would he hurry back up the hill? Or would he wait to see if they came down?

From their hiding place she could see very little, but she heard him coming. He was grunting and cursing with each step as if he was in agony, and pounding the ground with the cricket bat. That gave her satisfaction, at least. Perhaps if he did find them she could bash him on his wounded foot with something. She dug around in the undergrowth and found a fist-sized stone. If he came upon them she would go straight for his foot. She would smash it with the rock before he had a chance to defend himself.

He reached the campsite and she caught a glimpse of him through the ferns. Then the sounds stopped. Was he listening for them? She put a finger to her lips to keep Joey quiet, and tightened her hold on the rock. Then she heard him curse and start to shuffle away in the direction of the path that cut through the bush towards the O'Halloran farm.

For a heart-stopping moment she wondered if he might be going towards the pasture, but raising her head slightly she saw him disappear along the track into the bush towards the dairy farm. He had tied something around his left foot and was limping quickly without the cricket bat.

They remained in the ferns long enough to be sure he wasn't coming back and then held hands and stumbled towards the pasture. She had used almost all her strength and prayed that the boys would be able to do something.

Hemi and Niall had finished milking, and were sitting in the sun drinking milk from the billy and laughing together about something. They jumped up when they saw Mette and Joey, looking guilty. How sad to see them embarrassed about being happy. If only everything was normal and they were becoming friends without having to worry about how terrible life was right now.

"You're wet," said Niall. "Did you fall in the creek?"

"We jumped. Listen, both of you. Arthur killed Niall's father, and he tried to kill us - Joey and me. We have to find a place to hide until Frank returns. Where's the rabbit gun?"

Niall and Hemi glanced at each other. "Over there through the bush," said Hemi. "In Niall's hideaway. He showed me before. You can't see it. It's really hard to find."

"Take us there, then," she said. "As fast as you can."

She followed Niall through the bush to an area where the ground dropped sharply to the path along the fence. He helped her down the hill as she slid sitting down. With the climb down and the bumps from the stones in the creek, her bottom must be covered with bruises. To make matters worse, she kept expecting Arthur to appear along the path. But at least they were all together now, and just had to wait for Frank.

On the O'Halloran side of the fence by the path lay a pile of dead rabbits, looking as if they had been tossed there; some of the boiled oats that had killed them still remained on this side of the fence.

"Keep away from the oats, Joey."

"Is that what made Sergeant Frank sick?"

She nodded. "I expect this is where Arthur found the poison."

Niall stopped suddenly and said, "Here it is."

She couldn't see anything. "Where?"

They were beside a steep slope covered in scrub and ferns, at the top of which was a stand of trees with roots . Niall took two steps uphill, stopped, and pulled aside a branch. "In here. Let me give you a hand, Mrs. Hardy."

Feeling clumsy and ungainly, Mette grasped his hand and climbed up beside him. Wriggling through the gap she found herself in a tiny cave with barely enough room for them all. A roof of entwined branches and roots concealed them from the outside world.

She eased herself into a comfortable position and closed her eyes. She was exhausted, longing for sleep. But she had to keep the boys' spirits up. She opened her eyes and smiled at them. "I'm so glad you found this place, Niall. It's like a club house."

"We'll be safe here until Sergeant Frank returns," he said. He was becoming one of the family. She had called Frank 'Sergeant Frank' when she first met him, and Hemi and Joey had started using the name. Now here was Niall following suit. It was a long time since Frank had been a real sergeant, but once he started training the volunteers everyone called him that and it felt right. She was overcome with affection for all of them - Frank, her boys.

She put her arm around Joey and smiled at Niall and Hemi again. "Thank you so much for…"

Then her entire body was engulfed in the most terrible cramp. She put her hand on her belly and tried not to scream. This was not like the other cramps she had experienced. This was what her sister had talked about, the pain of a baby coming into the world. And at the most inconvenient time imaginable.

"Is something the matter Mrs. Hardy?"

The pain receded and she breathed once more. If it came again she would be in trouble. But Frank would be back soon, she was sure, and he would find someone to help her.

"Someone has to go down to the road and wait for Frank," she said. "And let him know where we are." She had hardly spoken when the pain came again. She clenched her teeth and doubled over, panting with the effort not to scream. "Ah, *min gut*. The baby's coming."

They stared at her, shocked.

"How do you…?" began Niall.

"I can feel…argh."

"I'll go and find Sergeant Frank," said Hemi. "I'm a fast runner. I'll get down to the road and run towards Feilding until I meet up with him."

"Take Sergeant Frank's gun," said Niall. "And your gun. We'll be safe here."

Hemi shook his head. "I have a pocket knife. And I can run faster than Arthur. I'll take Sergeant Frank's gun, though, because he has the ammo and will be able to use it. "

"Arthur won't be able to run very well. He has a hurt foot," said Joey. "Mumma stabbed him with the pitchfork."

"You've been very brave," said Hemi to Mette. "Now it's my

turn." He took a deep breath and stood up, the heavy rifle slung over one shoulder, his eyes closed, then he pushed himself up through the opening to the hideaway.

She watched as his thin brown legs rose out of sight. She had wanted to say something encouraging to him, but she was already in the throes of a third cramp and doing her best not to make a noise.

"I hope he finds Frank quickly," she said as the pain diminished again. She was speaking more for Niall and Joey than herself. How could Frank help her? He knew nothing about childbirth. He had ridden to fetch a midwife once, when Maren's twins were born, but other than that he would be no more use to her than Niall or Joey.

She was going to have to give birth to this baby by herself.

19

Frank Chases Arthur

His heart was pounding as he waded into the creek. What was he going to do if it was Mette? Throw himself into the water beside her? A howl was building in his chest and he had trouble breathing.

He reached the body and gathered it into his arms. She felt cold and lifeless, and her head flopped back over his elbow, her hair draped across her face and covering it.

"Mette. Mette. Are you alright?"

He lifted her hair gently from her face, his hand trembling with fear.

And realized he'd made a terrible mistake.

It wasn't Mette; it was Sarah. Somehow, she'd been released from her prison beneath the roots of the willow tree and been borne downstream. Her dress was no longer white, but darkened by mud. She had not been wearing the hat by accident. She had been propped up on the rock at the edge of the creek wearing Arthur's floppy, broad-brimmed hat on her head to make it look as if Arthur was sitting there. Arthur had set a trap for him, and he had walked into it. He was probably watching right now from somewhere.

His senses alert, he laid Sarah gently back in the water, pulled his gun from his belt and slipped back into the shadow of the overhanging willows. Sarah floated away from him and lodged against a rock, with one arm draped across it theatrically. He would come back for her later, unable to live with himself if he didn't give her a decent burial.

Where would Arthur hide? He didn't have a gun, but he'd been in prison for years and would know how to fight dirty, and how to fashion himself some kind of weapon. Somehow he had discovered his cover was blown and he was prepared to kill to cover up his identity. He doubted Arthur would stay hidden for long. He'd jump Frank at the first opportunity.

He stood still in the shadows, the fast-moving water tugging at his legs, and surveyed the area carefully. The creek was at its widest and deepest here, and almost impossible to cross. On the farm side of the creek, the trees were all willows, with narrow, drooping branches that did not afford good hiding places. The hydrangeas at the back of the house were long since flattened by the flood and beginning to rot. No place for anyone to hide there. The house was in even worse shape, with nothing remaining but the footings.

Copenhagen snickered, and he glanced towards her without moving. Had she seen something? Or heard something? John Brown's horse had sidled up to her and the pair were standing together as if in self-defence. Was Arthur in the barn? If so, where was John Brown?

Then he saw it. From a small window in the upper part of the barn, the tip of a rifle protruded, unwavering, pointing directly at him. In the shadows he'd be hard to see; he stayed still and watched to see if it moved. When he was sure it hadn't, he ran across the yard to the barn and stopped beside the horses. Looking up from his new position, he could see the barrel of the gun above him, unmoving. What the hell was going on? Who was up there? Was it Arthur, waiting for him but distracted by something or someone? Or had John Brown positioned himself up there and was maintaining silence, knowing Arthur was close by?

Arthur did not own a gun, but Frank's own gun was in the supply tent. He cursed himself for not taking it with him when he was at the campsite. But at least Arthur wouldn't have ammunition for the rifle; it was in Frank's pocket.

He scooped up a a handful of pebbles and tossed them towards the gun barrel. They clinked against it and fell in a shower around him. The barrel didn't waver, but stayed pointing towards the stream.

Leaving Copenhagen beside Brown's horse he entered the barn. It was small, not much more than fifteen feet across. A few barrels sat in one corner beside an old wooden chair with a bucket of oats on it. He checked behind the barrels. Nothing. Nowhere else to hide. In the centre of the room, a rickety ladder led up to a trapdoor. Feeling more and more apprehensive he climbed the ladder slowly and raised the trapdoor slightly. He could see the part of the room that faced away from the window. A pile of straw was heaped against the wall. He lifted the trapdoor higher, took out his watch and held it so he could see the other half of the room reflected in it. He could see a blurred figure on a box. He was wearing the blue regimental jacket that looked like the one John Brown had been wearing. Arthur's jacket was not blue. Not Arthur then.

He climbed through the trapdoor, relieved. John Brown

sat at the window, leaning forward, his rifle across his arm, watching someone on the other side of the yard.

"Thank God, Brown. I was wondering where the hell you were. Have you seen him?"

John Brown said nothing, and did not move. Frank crossed the room and touched him on the shoulder, understanding in his heart that something was wrong.

Brown fell backwards slowly, staring at Frank through sightless eyes. Frank caught him and lowered him to the floor. He was clearly dead, although there was no sign of a weapon. But the movement had caused a trickle of blood from the corner of his mouth. He'd been stabbed in the side of the neck as he looked out the window. With a knife, by the look of it, although the weapon had been withdrawn.

"Damn." He lifted the rifle from Brown's hands and checked it out. Empty. The cartridges had been removed.

He heard a rustling noise behind him, and spun around. Arthur was coming at him. Bits of straw clung to his clothing and he held the knife from Frank's carving set in both hands, raised for the kill.

Frank threw himself to one side, and felt Arthur trip on his shin and stumble towards the window. He landed on John Brown's body and rolled off, pushing it away angrily. Frank found himself staring into the dead man's eyes. He got to his knees and crawled away from the body. The hole where the ladder was propped was two feet away, and he threw himself towards it.

Before he was half way, Arthur landed on his back, grunting with effort as he tried to get his arm around Frank's neck. Frank dragged his arm loose, reared up onto his knees, and dumped Arthur backwards onto the floor. As Arthur struggled up, Frank dived head first down the ladder, his palms bumping against the rungs. He landed in a heap at the bottom, swung around, and kicked the ladder away. Arthur was right behind him at the top of the hole. He groped desperately for the ladder, missing it by inches.

"You're not getting away, you bastard."

Frank raised his revolver towards Arthur, who reared back out of sight.

He positioned himself outside the barn door, his revolver aimed at the door. No thought now of winging Arthur. When he came through the door he would drop him in his tracks. Time for him to die.

But Arthur surprised him. He heard a sound from above, and Arthur dropped from the window, using Frank to cushion his landing. The revolver flew from his hand and they fell to the ground, Arthur on top.

"Now I've got you." He slashed wildly at Frank with his knife.

Frank got a grip on Arthur's wrist and moved it away a few inches, but Arthur pushed back, slowly gaining control, his face red with concentration.

With their faces inches apart, they wrestled for control of the knife. Arthur was surprisingly strong, considering his build; Frank was unable to dislodge him or to move his knife hand away from his face. Once it came close enough to scratch his cheek, and would have taken an eye if Frank hadn't moved his head enough at the last minute to avoid the downward thrust. He managed to get Arthur's arm up again, and was straining as hard as he could, wondering if he would ever be free of Arthur, when Arthur rose away from him to the sound of a loud whack. Frank sat up, coughing, dazed by his good fortune.

Hemi stood there, Frank's rifle in hand, looking terrified. He was holding the rifle by the barrel, the wooden stock dangling on the ground.

Frank clambered to his feet and took the rifle from Hemi. He was winded and aching. "Good boy. Get behind me. I've got this."

Arthur was bleeding from the head. He looked stunned, but came at Frank with his knife one more time. Frank swung the rifle butt at him and missed when Arthur jumped away. He stood there staring at them both, then ran at the horses and vaulted astride John Brown's horse. He kicked at its side and galloped towards the lane, holding the knife aloft in one hand. Frank picked up his revolver and aimed it at the rapidly departing Arthur. He shot once, cursed, then shot again. But Arthur and his mount had disappeared down the lane between the poplar trees.

Frank bent over and got his breath back. He grabbed Copenhagen's reins and put one foot in the stirrup. "Hemi, I'm going after him. You…"

"You can't go, Sergeant Frank," said Hemi. He took hold of the reins and held them as Frank mounted her. "It's Mette. She needs you right now. I came to get you."

He tried to snatch the reins from Hemi, who clung to them. He was losing minutes as Arthur disappeared down the lane to the Feilding road. "She's safe for now. I'll be back as soon as I can. Let go of the reins."

"You can't leave. She's having a baby right now, and no one knows what to do. You have to come."

"What do you mean, she's having a baby right now? She isn't due for two more weeks."

"She's hurting. She keeps bending over like she's in pain. She sent me to get you. She said you'd know what to do."

He didn't know what to do. Was it something that could be delayed, or was there no choice? He knew absolutely nothing. But Mette had put her trust in him, and he was going to have to do his best. He jumped onto Copenhagen and pulled Hemi up behind him.

"Show me where to go."

20

The Hideaway

She was doomed to live with this awful pain forever. Niall and Joey had counted between contractions and had decided that the pains were still about five minutes apart. But five minutes passed so quickly, and gave her no relief. She wasn't sure what five minutes apart meant, but remembered Maren telling her that the pains were almost constant before the baby started to arrive. How she would know it was arriving, she had no idea. Maren hadn't said. Now she wished she'd asked her sister more about it, but at the time she had assumed there would be a midwife and lots of competent women around when it happened and they would tell her what to do.

Niall watched her anxiously, wincing in sympathy each time she doubled over. "Do you want me to help Hemi find Sergeant Frank?"

"He won't be able to do much more than you can," she said, panting as the pain receded. "Niall, if the baby comes, will you be able to help me? You knew what to do with the poison."

"I've read a lot of books on medicine," he said. "But not about babies. I used to help my father with the calving."

She seized on that. "It can't be much different."

He blushed and looked away. "I know how it looks when calves come out, Mrs Hardy. But I couldn't look at…"

"Maybe if the baby comes out by itself, you could pick it up and take care of it."

He nodded. "I suppose I could. But there's a cord…"

"What happens with that?"

"Well, the cow usually gnaws through it with her teeth."

She started to giggle. "I don't think I could…" A contraction interrupted her.

He waited until the contraction finished, and said, "I think I could do it with a knife, but we don't have one. Hemi said he has a pocket knife."

"Maybe you should find Hemi and tell him to come back." Joey said.

"I don't think I should leave," said Niall. "But you know what would help, Joey? For us to know what's going on outside. Stick your head out and see if you can see or hear anything. Be careful though. Don't let Arthur see you. Pull a branch or something over your head and stay very still."

As Joey poked his head cautiously through the hole, Niall whispered. "I thought it would be better if he didn't watch… for him as well as you."

She nodded and took a few deep breaths, which helped a little. "Could you talk to me about something - anything - to keep my mind off things? It's almost worse waiting for it to happen than having it happen. Tell me about Sarah."

"What would you like to know?"

"Did you like her?"

"I don't know. I hadn't spoken to her much until that last day. She liked nice clothes. My father gave her some money to buy some things at Lewers General Store in Feilding, and she was happy about that."

Mette was surprised. Perhaps Mr. O'Halloran was kinder than she had thought.

"But then he said she needed all the help money could buy to make her look nice enough to take her anywhere."

They waited out another contraction, then Mette asked, "And what about you? What makes you happy?"

He thought about it. "I like being by myself, and reading and thinking. But it's been good getting to know Hemi. We get along well, and he makes me laugh. It's like having a brother."

She reached out and took his hand. "You'll stay with us when this is all over, and you will be brothers."

He took his hand away from her, his face red. "That's very kind of you Mrs. Hardy. I have some things I'd like to do, and maybe you and Sergeant Frank could help me…"

"Do you want to be a doctor?"

He shook his head. "I want to be a vet - a veterinary surgeon, actually."

"That would be a very useful thing for you to do," she said. "Would you have to go to the university in Wellington?"

"England," he said. "The Royal Veterinary College in London. It takes three years and it's very expensive. My father thought it was a stupid idea. He said he had a good dairy herd and he needed me to help him with it. He said he wasn't going to throw away good money sending me off to stare at books for three years."

"I've always believed in education," said Mette. "For boys and girls, you…"

She stopped and waited until another contraction passed, realizing it had come sooner than the previous one. "My daughter will have an education, even university if she wants. And if she wants to be a doctor, she can be one."

"Will they let a girl be a doctor? Only, I've been reading about surgeries and they're a bit gruesome. Wouldn't a girl just faint if she had to do something like - well, I was reading the other day about surgery on a horse's eye and it sounded awful to me, but I can't imagine a girl being able to watch it, let alone do it herself. The surgeon cut a filaria from a horse's cornea. Do you know what a filaria is?"

Mette shook her head.

"It's a kind of round worm. It got into the animal's eye, and its eye was all cloudy. The surgeon had to put the horse to sleep - they made the horse drop on its side and gave it ether. Then the surgeon punctured the cornea with a lancet and held open the cut until the filaria came shooting out with the stuff that's inside an eye. It's kind of like a jelly. The filaria was over two inches long."

Mette was beginning to want a sniff of ether herself. "Did the horse survive?"

"It was quite old, for a horse. Nineteen years, I think. And you know with older horses how they get."

Joey ducked down from his perch and whispered, "I heard a shot."

They went quiet. Someone yelled and there was another shot followed by the thunder of hooves. It was hard to tell how far away it was or whether is was coming nearer of going away.

Mette propped herself up on one elbow. "It's Frank. Hemi must have found him. I hope they're alright."

Joey sat beside her and leaned against her, his elbow on her belly. She squeezed his arm. "We're going to be safe. Frank will be here soon."

But as she said it she felt a flood of wetness spurt between her legs and soak her skirt. It was followed by an overwhelming feeling that she had to push down hard to eject the baby.

Joey pulled his hand away from her belly, horrified. "Did I pop you?"

"Baby," she grunted. "Baby. Coming now."

Joey and Niall stared at her, speechless.

They heard the sound of hooves again, coming nearer. A horse was trotting along the path beside the fence. Niall slapped his hand over Joey's mouth, which he had opened as if he intended to yell. "Shh. Be quiet. We don't know who it is."

But Mette could no longer control herself. She gave a long, low howl and pushed down as hard as she could.

"Mette?"

Before Niall could stop him, Joey was on his feet and thrusting his head through the gap.

"Sergeant Frank?"

There was a scrabbling noise as someone climbed towards the hideaway, then Frank's anxious face appeared. "Was that Mette who screamed? Is she alright?"

"The baby's coming out," said Niall, his voice rising with panic. "It's coming out now. Sergeant Frank, you have to get down the other end and catch it."

He wriggled through the opening and manoeuvred around to face Mette. Hemi followed him through the opening and squeezed between Niall and Joey at her head. There was hardly any room for them, especially Frank, whose head scraped against the branches covering the cave. Mette had never seen such a look on his face in all the years she had known him. A look of pure terror and self-doubt.

189

But at least he was here. And they were all together. She gave another involuntary push and felt the baby start to emerge.

21

Birth and Death

For the first time in his life that he could remember, he had no idea what to do. Mette was in pain - no, not in pain, in agony - and he did not know how to help her. He reached back into the far recesses of his memory to the battlefields he had known, where men screamed as surgeons hacked off their limbs or scooped their intestines back into their guts, and groped for his belt. "Would you like to bite on this? It used to help..." She shook her head, her eyes closed, and gestured at him to put his belt away. He remembered the brandy in his pocket. "Take a sip of this."

She answered with another long, guttural scream, then panted, "Not alcohol. I don't need...lift up my dress. It's out."

The boys shrank back against the dirt wall of the hideaway; Frank took a swig of brandy and lifted her dress.

"Think of a horse giving birth, or a cow," said Niall. He was watching Frank intently, in control of his fear now that Frank was here and he was no longer in charge. "It's sort of the same. And once it's out her pain will disappear."

Frank could see the top of the head. He put his hands beneath it and waited. Mette grunted and he could see her pushing hard with her whole body. The rest of the baby slid out and landed in his shaking hands. "I've got him. He's out. We need something to wrap him in."

Hemi pulled his shirt over his head and shoved it towards Frank. "Take this."

He wrapped his child in the shirt, wishing he had one of the gowns Mette had lovingly folded into the chest back at the house. Hemi had been wearing the shirt for a week, and it was covered with grass stains and specks of mud. He pulled it away from the child's face and stared at it. Dark hair, angry red face, full pursed lips like Mette's. He'd done it.

"Give him your knife," Niall said to Hemi. "He needs to cut the cord. Pour some brandy over it to clean it."

Frank took the knife, doused it in brandy, and, holding the baby by the head and supporting its body with his forearm, he carefully cut the cord that attached it to Mette, as near to the child as he could. He returned the knife to Hemi and attempted to tie the end of the cord into a knot with his uncooperative fingers. As he did, he noticed something.

"It's not a boy. It's a girl."

Joey put his hands to his mouth and started to giggle. "A girl," he said. "Does that mean I have a sister?"

"Me too," said Hemi. "Can I hold her while you clean her up?"

"Her? Which her...oh, you mean while I clean up Mette?" He handed the baby to Hemi, who held her against his bare chest, grinning down at her, while Frank poured brandy on Mette, and then pulled her skirt down.

"She looks like you, Sergeant Frank."

Mette gave a deep sigh and lifted her head. "Can I see her?"

Hemi wriggled round beside her and laid the baby on Mette's shoulder. "Here she is. Look at her hands. Her fingers are so tiny. You can almost see through them."

Mette clutched the baby to her cheek. "She isn't breathing."

Frank took his daughter gingerly. "She isn't." He shook her gently. "She should be, shouldn't she?" he asked Niall.

"Breath into her mouth."

He was afraid he would do something wrong, but he blew gently into her mouth and saw her chest rise and fall a few times. When he stopped, she made a spluttering sound and started to cry, a thin, high-pitched squeal that made the boys cover their ears. He put her back on Mette's shoulder, wiped his forehead and polished off the rest of the brandy in one gulp.

"God, that was terrifying."

Mette stroked her new daughter's hair, and said softly, "She's beautiful. She has so much hair and it's so dark."

"Are you feeling better now?" Frank put his hand on her free shoulder. "I thought you weren't going to make it for a while there."

"It wasn't that bad," she said. She put her little finger in the baby's mouth and smiled as she sucked it loudly. "I think I should give her my breast."

Frank saw the looks on the boys' faces. "Let's get everything sorted out first. We'll get out of here and back to the campsite. One of the boys can run down to the house and get your other dress and something to wrap the baby in."

"Are we safe now? What happened to Arthur?"

"Arthur is the bad man," said Joey. "Did you know that Sergeant Frank? He tried to kill us, but we jumped into the creek and got away."

He nodded. "I tracked you to the stream. The Feilding police told me about Arthur. He's not a ticket-of-leave man. He was, but he got involved with a group of bushwhackers in Melbourne and was sent back to prison. Then he escaped during the fuss over the hanging of Ned Kelly, and made his way to the port. He killed a ship's cook so he could take his place and came to New Zealand where no one knew him. Or at least, where he hoped no one knew him. I think he wanted to use our place as a bolt hole. That's why he tried to poison us - so he could stay here without worrying about anyone going for help."

Mette sighed and moved her body awkwardly, trying to keep the baby where she was on her shoulder. In spite of what she said, he could tell she was still in some discomfort. "Do Mr. and Mrs. Burns know about Arthur? They're not in prison, I hope."

"Constable Price had them in a hotel room, but the solicitor will be on his way and they'll be freed. He's bringing a posse. They'll be here soon."

"Arthur's gone, then?"

"Hemi and I chased him off. He took Niall's horse, and was heading towards Feilding. He'll probably run right into Constable Price and his posse."

"I hit him with the butt of the rifle," said Hemi. "He was going to kill Sergeant Frank with the carving knife."

"You did well, Hemi," said Frank. "Thank you for saving me. I don't know what started all this, or why he felt he needed to kill Mr. O'Halloran."

"It was about my book," said Joey. "Remember I showed you the drawing and I kept saying it looked like Arthur? Well, it *was* Arthur. He tried to murder the Queen of England and Mr.

O'Halloran was there and remembered him."

"Hemi dropped his book in front of Arthur and it fell open," said Mette. "I picked it up, and when I saw the drawing, I knew…"

"I followed your steps," said Frank. "I could see that you and Joey had jumped into the creek to get away from Arthur. That must have been terrifying."

"Joey jumped in the creek? And he can't even swim? " said Hemi. "That was brave, Joey."

Frank ruffled Joey's hair. "You've been a trooper throughout this whole ordeal, Joey. I'm proud of you. I'm proud of you all."

"Do you think we could get out of my hideaway now?" asked Niall. "It's sort of warm and stinky in here. Like a barn. If Arthur's gone and the posse is on its way we should be safe, shouldn't we?"

"I'll go first," said Frank. "Once I'm sure it's safe, the rest of you can follow me out. Make sure you help Mette, and be careful with the baby."

"Sarah Jane," said Mette. "I'm going to call her Sarah Jane, so they can both be remembered."

He eased himself slowly from the hideaway. His gut ached and the cut on his face was starting to bleed. He felt completely exhausted, his entire body bruised. Thank God they were all safe. All he needed now was rest. In the distance he heard the faint sounds of men and horses. The posse was here.

He pulled back the hammer of his revolver and spun the cylinder. He had two shots left.

"I hear the posse," he said to the group in the hideaway. "I'm going to shoot to attract their attention. Block your ears."

He raised his gun and shot upwards, away from the sounds so the bullet wouldn't come down near them. Then he slid down the hill to the pathway.

Where Arthur was waiting for him, one hand on Copenhagen's saddle. She had her head down, eating hungrily from the edge of the path. It had been a while since she had been fed.

"Hello sergeant. Are you looking for your horse? I thought you might be, so I brought her with me. Sorry Mrs. Hardy was upset, but she seems to have survived her trip down the creek. She's quite the woman - but I suppose you know that."

Frank could not keep his eyes off Copenhagen, who was finishing the last of the poisoned oats. "What the hell have you done to my horse?"

Arthur shrugged. "She was hungry. What can I say?"

He levelled his gun at Arthur. "Get away from my horse, or I'll shoot you in the leg and make sure you'll never walk again." Even as he said it, he knew his days of hurting other people were over. He was sick at the thought shooting anyone.

Arthur smiled sadly. "You think I don't want to die? I spent ten years in Pentridge. I'm not going back. You know what they do there? They torture you. They put hoods over your head and leave you sitting in your cell for days on end, with only bread and water. They think that's more effective than beating you with a rod or the cat and less cruel. It isn't. It can drive you mad. I wasn't always a killer, you know. It was prison made me that way."

"You don't have to worry about torture," said Frank. He started to ease towards Arthur. How much time did he have? How much time did Copenhagen have? The voices of the posse were coming closer, accompanied by the sounds of horse hooves pounding on the dirt. "They're going to hang you anyway, either here or back in Australia. Get away from my horse."

Arthur moved his hand from Copenhagen's saddle. He was holding a knife - the small one from the wedding gift set. He bent down, his knife-hand propped on his knee, and inspected the ground beside Copenhagen. "She's been eating it the whole time," he said. "It's all gone. She won't last much longer. You can watch us both die."

Still smiling, he raised the knife and slashed himself across the throat. Blood spurted out towards Frank. He put up his arm to prevent it hitting him in the face, and ran towards Copenhagen, throwing Arthur to one side. She whinnied, pressed her muzzle against Frank's shoulder, then slowly sank to her knees, dragging him down with her

Frank cradled her head. It was too late, he knew. She shuddered a few times, then began to twitch and foam at the mouth, roaring loudly. He knew that was the sound of extreme pain. Her eyes pleaded with him to make it stop. After a few more minutes, he put his gun against her temple, closed his eyes, and pulled the trigger. Then he crossed his arms on his knees, sank his head onto his arms, and wished he had saved a bullet for himself.

He heard the boys scrambling down from the hideaway. Mette must have come with them somehow. She said nothing, but sat beside him and put her arms around him, cradling the baby between them. Sarah Jane he supposed he should call her now. But he was unable to move. A black mist had taken over his mind and he thought he would never be happy again.

"You got him, did you?" said Constable Price several minutes later. He was accompanied by the assistant constable and three large Scandinavians carrying axes. He and his assistant both held rifles at the ready.

Frank raised his head. "He got himself," he said, his voice rasping. "Slashed his throat with my carving knife. You'll find more bodies as well. James O'Halloran in a rolled up tent at our campsite. His wife beside the creek near the remains of his house. And John Brown in the loft of the barn. I'm sorry about Brown. I believe Arthur thought it was me."

"What happened to your horse?"

"Poisoned," said Frank. "He was trying to force me to kill him. Said he didn't want to go back to prison in Australia."

"Ah," said Constable Price. "Suicide by copper, we call that. Just as well you let him kill himself. No need to have that on your conscience."

22

Regeneration

Constable Price assigned a Scandinavian railway worker to escort Mette and the baby to her sister's place in Bunnythorpe, and they left Feilding in a dray without a backward glance, Mette wearing her second best dress and the baby bundled in a knitted cap and shawl, fast asleep on Mette's lap. Frank knew she assumed she would see him later in the day and didn't tell her that she would not.

He barely managed to see her off before the black mood descended on him fully. He went to the bar at the Feilding Hotel and had a couple of stiff drinks with Jeremiah Burns, who was surprisingly sanguine about what Frank had put him through.

"I'm going to make some changes in our lives," Burns said. He took a long gulp of his ginger beer. "I'll sell the farm and move to Feilding so that Grace will have more to keep her occupied. She has friends here and she won't need to spend her time alone. And there'll be people around she knows if anything happens to me."

That got Frank thinking. After Burns had gone to his room

to tend to his wife, he sat at the bar and had a few more drinks by himself, wondering what would happen to Mette and the baby - God knows why she had called her Sarah Jane, after a dead woman and a dead baby - if something happened to him.

He awoke the next morning feeling like hell, his head throbbing, his mouth dry, and every muscle in his body aching. He sat on the bed and made a plan.

The first thing he was going to do was take the pledge. Not the full pledge, but from now on he would limit himself to a beer or two a day. He had given up smoking for Mette. He could give up drinking. Then he would get himself back in fighting condition, so that if anything like this ever happened again he would be better able to handle it. Although he was glad that Hemi had saved him from Arthur, he was also embarrassed that it had been necessary. And he could scarcely bear the thought that he had been responsible for the death of John Brown.

Next on the list was a will, which he did not have. He dressed, ate a quick breakfast, and went to find Mr. Goodbehere, the solicitor who had defended Grace Burns.

Mr. Goodbehere, a sturdy, grey-bearded man in his early sixties, pumped Frank's hand with two quick up and down strokes. Frank had not recognized the name, but he recognized the man; he had seen him watching cricket matches. When he mentioned that to Goodbehere, he nodded and commented that he usually watched his son, Edmund's matches. Frank would have seen him there.

Asked if he could leave his property to Mette, Goodbehere folded his hands on his desk and nodded. "You could, of course. But do you have any children? A son, perhaps?"

"A daughter," said Frank. He had no intention of telling

Goodbehere about his unacknowledged son, who lived in the South Island on his own 30,000 acre property.

"How old?"

"One day," said Frank.

"Ah then, not the best alternative. You're not even sure, as yet, that she'll survive infancy. A brother, perhaps?"

Frank had to admit that no, he didn't have a brother. His only brother had died in the Land Wars.

Goodbehere sighed and shook his head. "In that case you must leave everything to your wife. Although of course, according to the Act, any money she earns herself would be her own and you don't need to leave her that. Does she make butter, or anything along those lines?"

Frank shook his head, but remembered the recipe pamphlets Mette had sold through Mr. Robinson when she worked for him at the book shop, and the letters she had written for illiterate Danish and German immigrants. He would find her something to work at so she could have her own money. And she would want Joey taken care of. As much as he tried, he could still not warm to Joey and his timidity. At least Hemi was growing into a man.

"And is there a man you could trust to make sure your wife did not act foolishly...by remarrying the wrong person, for example? A good, solid Englishman if possible?"

Frank mentally crossed Hop Li off his list. He did have an idea that he'd been tossing around, and he told Goodbehere what it was, without all the details. Goodbehere agreed it was a reasonable option, and said they could discuss it the following day, after Frank had talked to the young man in question. "I'll see you tomorrow, after the funerals," he said.

The funerals of James and Sarah O'Halloran were the next morning. James O'Halloran had purchased a grave site for himself at the Feilding Cemetery, and he and his wife were laid, one on top of the other, in the single grave.

Frank stood with Niall as the coffins of his father and stepmother were lowered into the ground. Niall stared at the ground with a bitter smile on his face as his stepmother was placed on top of his father.

"I hope she spends eternity weighing on him," he said to Frank, without looking up.

"Niall, I've been thinking about what we should do with you for the next few years."

Niall's glanced at him. "Do with me? What do you mean?"

"I have a suggestion. Mette told me that you want to go to the Royal Veterinary College in London. I looked into it and you'll need to study with a tutor for a couple of years before you can even apply. I'll find you one in Wellington, and we'll set you up there. Most tutors offer room and board."

"How will I pay for it? I mean, my father was always saying how poor he was. Where's the money going to come from?" He kicked at the dirt beside his father's open grave. "It's exactly what I'd like to do, though, if it's possible."

"I'll pay for it. I'm going to become your legal guardian. You'll give me your farm…"

"Give you my farm? That doesn't sound right."

"Hear me out," said Frank. "You give me your farm, and I'll pay for everything and give you a stipend until you can earn for yourself. When I die you'll get your farm back. By then I'll have it in good shape. It will be an investment for you."

"What about Mette? What does she think about this? And will you put Sarah Jane in your will?"

He didn't think that was any of Niall's business, but didn't say so. "Don't worry about it. I don't intend to die just yet." Secretly, Goodbehere's suggestion that he should wait to see if his daughter survived infancy had shocked him. He had blocked all thought of putting her in his will after that. It would be like tempting fate.

"And what about Hemi and Joey?"

"Mette will take care of them. I can trust her to do that. So what do you think? Are you willing to sign your farm over to me, on my promise to return it to you in my will?"

Niall stared at the grave as if he would like to hear his father's opinion. "I don't know. If you think it's a good idea, I suppose I trust you. I like the idea of having a family. I will have a family, won't I?"

Frank stared at the hills in the distance for several minutes, and then said, "But I'll only do all this on one condition."

"What's that?"

"That you tell me the truth about Sarah. Tell me what really happened to Sarah."

When Niall's face turned bright red, Frank knew he'd guessed correctly.

"I...I..."

"Tell me, Niall. You didn't murder anyone, but your story doesn't add up. And I think I know what happened. So you may as well tell me if I'm right. You slept with her, didn't you?"

Niall nodded, his face now long and sad. "I...we..yes I did."

"Walk with me, and tell me the whole story."

They walked towards Cemetery Road, where they had left their horses. "Where should I start?"

"Tell me about you and Sarah first. Then how your father found out and when he hit you."

Niall sighed. "I used to listen to them at night, through the wall. It made me feel...I don't know, excited."

Frank nodded. When he'd been Niall's age, he remembered, all he ever thought about was women. He was not much older when he'd been sent to rescue the daughter of someone important after the Siege of Lucknow, in India. He'd been thrown together with an older woman, and that had led to the conception of his son Milo.

"And I think she liked what they were doing, but she didn't like him. He wasn't kind to her."

"When was the first time you were together? Was it the first day of the flood?"

Niall bit his lip, and Frank waited. "A few weeks before that. It was like I said. She came into my room and wanted to cuddle, because she was homesick. And the next thing I knew we were..."

"So the child was yours?"

"I don't know. But she stopped sleeping with my father. She told him she couldn't stand him any more. That's why he bought her the white dress and the nightdress. He was trying to make it up to her. But she told me she wanted to leave. She couldn't stay with him any longer. She asked me if I'd help her get away, and I said I would."

"And what happened on the day I came down to your place?"

"My father went out to the barn, like I said, and Sarah came into my room. She only came in to show me the white dress he had bought for her. She was wearing her nightdress and she took it off. We were in my bed together and we heard him coming up the front steps. I jumped up and dragged the two bags of corn into the room and put them against the door. She put on the white dress and threw the nightdress on top of the sack, and we climbed out the window. But as I slammed it shut, the sash broke."

The window had been down that first time, and when he went back with Niall, it had been opened. He would see what Niall had to say about that.

"I took her up the creek towards your place. I told her to seek shelter with you and that I would come up later and we would run away together. I don't know how we were going to do it. She didn't either. But we were happy we were doing something."

They reached the horses and Niall stood with his hand on the saddle. He looked sad.

"I went back down and came around the other side of the house so he'd think I'd been that way. He asked me where Sarah was, and I told him I'd taken her down the creek towards the Feilding road, and that she was going to walk into Feilding."

"You wanted to give her a chance to get away, and to mislead him," said Frank.

"Yes. He was in the house, pushing on the door. I went in and he asked me where she was, and when I said where she'd gone - well, where she hadn't gone - he hit me. We got the horses and went after her. We didn't find her, of course, because we went the wrong way."

"And when you returned, I was there."

Niall nodded. "I didn't have a chance to do anything about the window or the sacks in my room, but when you sent me to find my father, I went back to the house, moved the sacks, and propped open the window with my ruler. Then I threw the sacks out. I didn't want my father to work out what had happened."

"How did you get into the room? I tried to push the door

open but couldn't."

"I climbed through the rafters and over the wall," said Niall. "It's open at the top, you know. Didn't you notice? And then I heard you coming and came out. I was more worried about you than about my father at that stage. I thought you'd work out what I'd done, but you didn't."

Frank shook his head. "I didn't, did I?"

"But you suspected what had happened…"

"Not really. I just knew something wasn't right with you or your story."

"Do you still want me to inherit the farm?"

"Half the farm," said Frank. "Which is really yours anyway. Yes I do. Tell me something. Were you in love with Sarah, or was it just about the intercourse?"

"I liked her. I thought she was pretty…sort of pretty. She had white skin and red hair, which is why my father didn't like her. He thought she looked too Irish. Do you think the dog scared her? It wasn't Arthur, was it?"

"I think it most probably was the dog," said Frank. "I saw her body, and she looked perfect. No marks or wounds anywhere on her. She looked very pretty in the coffin, with her red hair draped beside her face."

Niall put his head on the horse and started to cry. "I told you it was my fault she died. I was right, wasn't I?"

Frank couldn't answer. He was thinking, red hair, not fair, like Mette. But Frank had seen the way Niall looked at Mette, and he was going to have to put an alternative of some kind in place to make sure Niall didn't think he could worm his way into Mette's heart.

23

Looking to the Future

February 1881

Mette had been living with her sister Maren for two months while Frank repaired the farm. She'd seen him regularly on Sundays, when he took a half day off from his work and came with them to church. She comforted him as much as she could, but his mood was dark and he seemed afraid to look at or touch Sarah Jane, as if his touch was cursed. Then, three weeks ago, he had stopped coming altogether.

She had learned everything from Maren she hadn't realized she needed to know, having had no idea a baby required so much attention. She'd assumed babies mostly slept and ate, sleeping during darkness and eating three times a day, like a normal person. Instead, she'd discovered she spent all her time putting Sarah Jane to bed, getting her up when she cried two hours later, feeding her, burping her, putting her back to bed, and so on. It never ended. She was exhausted. But she loved her new daughter more than she had ever thought possible, and wished she could share her new-found emotions with Frank.

She knew Frank had been cleaning and fixing their house and the farm, making everything ready for their return as a family, but he had told her very little. Niall and Hemi were helping him, while Joey stayed with her at Maren's house. Fortunately, Pieter, who was doing extremely well with his dairy herd, had enlarged the house to make room for his growing family, and there was space for Mette and Joey at the moment; Maren was not pregnant for the first time in years and all the children had a place to sleep, the girls in one room and the boys in another. Mette and Joey shared the room her sister kept for visitors, with Sarah Jane in a bassinet beside them. But she missed Frank terribly and was a little angry with him for not letting her know what was going on.

She was almost at the point of commandeering the trap and horse and riding out to the farm with the baby, when he turned up one morning in the middle of the week on his new horse, Meteor, looking less wild than he had when she last saw him, with his hair brushed and his beard trimmed.

"I'm going to leave Meteor here and drive you over to the farm in the trap," he said. "I have something to show you."

Wrapping Sarah Jane in her shawl, she pulled herself onto the seat of the trap, refusing his help. After eight weeks hefting the baby around her arms were starting to look like his, without the tattoos. She didn't need his help.

They drove in near silence to the farm. She asked him once if he felt any better, and he said he did. He had buried Copenhagen at the edge of the pasture and went there sometimes to contemplate the past.

The track behind their house was filled in with logs and

covered over with gravel and dirt, and they were able to go from Bunnythorpe to Awahuri without going through Feilding. But as she arrived at the farm gate, she felt a shudder of revulsion run through her body and wondered if she would ever again be happy in her own house. The memory of Arthur telling her he was going to kill her and Joey came back to her with a jolt.

The feeling was worse inside the house. Frank and the boys had cleaned it thoroughly, but she was unable to enter their bedroom. She stood at the door, frozen to the spot, and pressed her face against Sarah Jane's head.

Frank laid his hand on her shoulder and squeezed. "It's difficult, isn't it?"

She nodded and leaned back against him. "I can't sleep in that bed again," she said. "Or that room. I'll have nightmares."

"You don't have to. I burned the bed. Let's go up to the high paddock. I have something to show you."

As they left the house, he scooped up a heavy-looking haversack that was leaning against the door jamb and slung it onto his back.

"Is that a surprise of some kind?"

It would take more than a surprise gift to make her forget what she had been through.

He opened the sack and showed her what was inside.

"Bricks?"

"I've been running up and down to the high paddock with this on my back, trying to get myself back into fighting condition. I think it's working. I'm stronger than I used to be."

She laughed. "Like me, carrying Sarah Jane around. I could probably carry that pack on my hip as easily as you can on your back."

"I think I prefer carrying bricks. At least I know I can toss it around. I'm too worried that I'll drop the baby and hurt her."

She noticed he had still not called the baby by name. "You get used to it."

"I think I'll wait until she can walk. When will that be?"

"Another year. You'll have to carry her around before then."

He smiled and shrugged. "I suppose so."

At the campsite, she was less nervous and shaky than she had been at the house. But she was surprised that they could now see all the way down to the river, the view they had previously only seen from the seat in the ridge.

"You've been cutting down trees?"

He nodded. "Come and sit down over here."

They sat on a log together where they had once sat around the fire, and where Frank had drunk the milk with the poison. It gave her a little twinge of anxiety, but she was able to push it away. The fact that she could now see such a broad vista was also calming. She took a deep breath and asked, "What did you want to show me?"

He waved his hand at the area between the campsite and the missing trees. "This," he said. "This is where we're going to build our new house."

"But…"

"It's going to be a bigger house than the old one, with eight rooms and an upper storey. Joey and Hemi will have a room on one side of the house, and we'll have our room on the other side." A small smile flitted across his face. "So we can't hear each other."

"What are we going to do with the other house? It seems such a waste."

"I've hired a farm manager. He's just out from England - a new chum - and he has a wife and young son. He's had a lot of experience with race horses and he's very keen to move in as soon as he can. He'll keep Hemi on as an assistant, and train him."

"Is that what Hemi wants to do?"

"It was his idea. He wants to be a jockey and our new manager has promised he'll do his best to find him mounts. He's excited about it, and it will keep him away from the Front. I've been worried about that. He's old enough now to go to war like his father."

She had a thousand questions, but knew the first one was the most important.

"How can we afford this? A new house and a manager? We barely make enough to support ourselves."

He laid his arm across her shoulders and stared straight ahead. Something was coming that he didn't expect her to like.

"Well, Dolores had her foal, so that helped. I sold it at the sales last week and did very well - and the yearling colt. I sold that as well. And I entered a couple of Rifle Association matches to give me some cash in hand while I wait for the insurance. Won fifty quid at one of them. But the important part of the plan is that we live in Wellington for a year. I know you'll miss Maren and her children, and your friends in Palmerston and Feilding, but it's the only way. We'll spend the year saving as much as we can to build the new house and pay the farm manager. When the house is ready we'll come back."

Mette was not as upset as he seemed to expect. In fact, she liked the idea. "Wellington? That will be alright, I suppose. But I still don't know where all the money will come from. And where will we live in Wellington?"

"I found us a little place on Majoribanks Street on Mount Victoria. A cottage, only fifteen shillings a week. It has a small garden and a nice verandah looking onto the street. I think you'll like it."

"Fifteen shillings a week - that's over a hundred pounds a year."

"Two things," he said. "And I hope you don't mind me promising that you'll do something. I was with Mr. and Mrs. Burns last week. Mrs. Burns was touched that you'd named the baby after her girl. She says she's very fond of you. She hasn't taken laudanum for two months, and believes you were the one who helped her stop. They wanted to repay you..."

"We can't take money from the Burnses."

"Not take money. Work. Remember them talking about their friends, the Halcombes? Mrs. Halcombe is an artist, and she's recently put together a book of her paintings. She's been wanting to publish the book in Germany, as books about New Zealand are popular there. She needs a translator..."

She was surprised. Frank was asking her to earn money for the family, which she'd always wanted to do. "I can do that. I'd love to do that. But I'm very busy with Sarah Jane, and tired most of the time."

"I hired a nurse maid for you. The woman renting us the cottage has a fifteen-year-old daughter who's looking for work. She's a bright young thing and strong. Bridget, her name is. She has red hair and freckles, and a broad Irish accent. I think Niall..."

"Are you matchmaking for Niall?"

He shook his head, looking guilty for some reason. What was wrong with matchmaking?Mette liked the idea of having a bright young thing named Bridget to help her with Sarah-

Jane. And of working on a translation. Perhaps there would be more translation work, once she had finished the book for Mrs. Halcombe. She was quite excited at the prospect. She'd loved working in the book shop before she was married, and had found that being at home with nothing to do but cook and garden had slowed down her brain, as much as she liked having her own vegetable garden.

"And what will you be doing while I'm taking care of Sarah Jane and working on a translation?"

"That's the big advantage of moving to Wellington. Constable Price showed me a copy of the *Evening Post* a few weeks ago with a list of tenders from the Armed Constabulary at the Mount Cook Barracks in Wellington, where they're headquartered. They were looking for someone to procure extra horses for the mounted constables massing at the Front. It's a twelve-month contract, and it pays very well."

"That sounds perfect for you. But you won't have to go to the Front, will you?"

He shook his head. "I've told them I won't. At the most, I'll help with transportation aboard ships. Then I'll turn around and come back, without disembarking. And I'll be at home more than I'm away. Do you think you'll be happy? I've been worrying that you'll hate it."

Sarah Jane began rooting at her breast, and without thinking, she opened her blouse and began feeding her. "I think it sounds nice for a year. And what about Joey? He'll come to Wellington with us of course. And Niall. I feel responsible for him now, and he isn't old enough to stay by himself. Will he come to live with us in Wellington?"

He stared at his hands, temporarily at a loss for words for some reason. "I'm Niall's legal guardian now. We've joined our farms into one - legally - and I sold the herd to cover his expenses for the next few years. I've put him in my will so he'll get his own land back when I die. And of course Joey and Hemi will be taken care of as well. Especially Joey. He seems less able to care for himself than Hemi."

She felt a faint stab of annoyance. Poor Joey. Would Frank never come around to him? He seemed to have a better plan for Niall's future. "And will Niall expect a home in Wellington?"

"He'll visit us occasionally, but he won't be living with us, no. Best not, I think. He says he'd like to be part of our family. He has no one else. I thought you wouldn't mind."

She detached Sarah Jane from her breast. If Niall was part of what Frank considered his family, he was going to have to understand that Sarah Jane was also part of his family.

Before he could object, she thrust the baby at him. "Here. Take Sarah Jane. Put her against your shoulder."

He took her awkwardly. "I don't want to drop her."

"You won't. Pretend she's a rugby ball."

He held her against his chest with one hand on her head and the other on her bottom.

"That's the way. Now rub her back."

He rubbed her back obediently, and sniffed her head.

"She smells nice."

Sarah Jane belched loudly and spat up on Frank's shoulder.

He held his daughter under her armpits, his arms extended from the elbow, and stared at her nervously. "What..look what she did? Is she sick? What's the matter with her?"

Sarah Jane examined him with clear brown eyes, a youthful version of his own. Then her face split in a lopsided, drunken smile as a bubble of spit grew between her lips and popped.

Frank started to laugh. Sarah Jane joined him, her laugh

sounding like a rusty saw cutting through a log.

"That's the first time I've heard her laugh," said Mette.

He stood up, smiling broadly, holding Sarah Jane close to his chest - to his heart.

"Sarah Jane, let me show you where you're going to sleep in our new house," he said. "Then we'll see where we will keep your pony. And I'm going to show you how to play cricket. You need to learn how to catch a ball if you have any hope of success in life. Even a girl should know how to throw a ball."

Mette wiped away a tear of relief. "Perhaps we should wait until she can walk before we buy her a pony or a cricket bat."

But Frank was busy showing his daughter where she was going to ride her rocking horse, and didn't hear her.

THE END

24

Afterword

Arthur O'Connor really did try to assassinate Queen Victoria in 1872 in the manner mentioned in this book. And John Brown did jump from the carriage to foil the attempt (see more about John Brown and his interesting relationship with Queen Victoria in the movie Mrs. Brown. Arthur O'Connor was sent to Australia, and what happened to him after that is unclear. He did not go to New Zealand, however. I took creative licence with that.

Laudanum was a major problem for Victorian woman, rivalling the current opioid epidemic. And there was at least one case in New Zealand where a woman was charged with infanticide when she used laudanum on her baby's gums, accidentally killing it. The patent medicines used at that time, even those given to babies, often contained laudanum or alcohol.

Note that anything Mette uses tends to be an older version of something we might use now. Willow bark has a similar chemical makeup to aspirin, and the honey she uses from the manuka bush has natural antibacterial qualities, according to WebMD. You can buy it in your local supermarket, but the good stuff is very expensive. Keep in mind that Mette is almost always right.

I'm working on a new book now and hope to have it finished in a few months (September 2020, perhaps). It's based on two related true stories: the robbery of gold bullion from the steamship Tararua in 1880, and the subsequent disaster when the same ship sank with major loss of life in 1881. Both Mette and Frank will survive, of course, but not before they have some difficult times.

Eventually Sarah Jane will have her own series. She'll be off to South Africa during the Boer War, and later will be involved with the Spanish Flu pandemic.

If you haven't read the earlier books, you can find the complete Sergeant Frank Hardy Mysteries series on all the popular sites. Search for *Not the Faintest Trace*, *Recalled to Life*, *Dead Shot*, and the novella *A Dark and Painful Mystery*.

I hope everyone is keeping well.

Wendy